An Apprentice Dictator in the White House

An Apprentice Dictator in the White House

Abner Clerveaux

abcbook16@gmail.com
www.abcbook16.com

Library of Congress Control Number: 2016912626
ISBN: Hardcover   978-1-5245-3147-8
               Softcover   978-1-5245-3146-1
               eBook   978-1-5245-3145-4

Print information available on the last page.

Rev. date: 08/05/2016

To order additional copies of this book, contact:
Xlibris
1-888-795-4274
www.Xlibris.com
Orders@Xlibris.com
745433

CONTENTS

Author's Notes

As an informed observer, I advise statesmen and women, especially in so-called law-abiding countries, to be careful and avoid extramarital affairs since they can lead to huge scandals, which the press love dealing with.

Indeed, in the cities where they live, these representatives must avoid being seen as cheaters.

If they are unfortunately caught committing this crime, their constituents would be offended, and the media would make a real commotion out of it.

Maybe not knowing the saying, "The spirit is willing, but the flesh is weak," some open-minded people would say on the contrary that there is no need to blame the head of state in developed countries for cheating because the leader of the nation is also a human being, and as a matter of fact, no human character should be unknown to him.

They unknowingly and inadvertently translated a saying by the Latin author named Terence that goes, *Homo sum, nihil a me humani alienum puto* ("I am human, and nothing of that which is human is alien to me.")

If we recognize that philosophy as an absolute truth, why should we keep treating a head of state as a criminal for extramarital affairs to the point that the parliament can turn itself into a high court of justice to prosecute and threaten him with destitution?

Congressmen and senators ought to reconsider and avoid in the future trying to impeach a newly elected president for a reason that's considered by some as bogus.

In Third World countries, unfortunately there are too many of them. These types of events are quite common. They don't even catch the press or the people's attention.

Could it be that Third World counties are considered as pariah states with low sense of morality?

One is free to have their own opinion according to their education or, specifically, one's ways and customs, which can be quite controversial depending on where you are in the world. However, according to "Christian morality," polygamy is rejected, if not completely banned.

It goes even further and claims that lusting over another man's wife is a crime. The fact of desiring her makes us sinners in the heart. Therefore, would it not be better for a man to only be devoted to his wife regarding matters of the flesh, without never trying to seduce someone else's?

By doing so, he would avoid violent reactions by his wife, who of course, out of jealousy or maybe out of love for her husband, would not want to share him with anyone.

Restraint remains the best attitude here. It doesn't matter if you are upper class, middle or lower class.,.

If I remember well, this kind of aberration happened and was largely talked about in one of the greatest countries on earth.

The guilty personality who confessed his sins was then judged by the parliament then elevated into the high court. But quite luckily, he very closely escaped destitution. Now the personality in question, the occupant of the White House, feeling hunted by his political enemies, has released his dictatorial claws.

The following lines will tell you about what happened behind the scene at the White House.

You are urged to follow the drama that is about to play.

PREAMBLE

This is a fictional paradox that doesn't answer to the truth but could have happened. It's a credible story because the mind of the politician, leader of the greatest nation on earth, almost in its entirety, is haunted by the will to act as he sees fit regardless of the legislative and judicial powers.

Such behavior is not unknown throughout history and once had been commonplace. However, over the years, tyranny as a form of government tends to be hated.

Therefore, know that no one who would introduce such parody of government at the White House could be perceived in this country of democratic tradition as a model of a democrat.

Thank God I was able to be at the right place at the right time as an eyewitness to this saga in order to warn the world leaders who want to take ownership of all the powers.

However, to the contrary, they'd better make cautiousness a cardinal virtue because in general, the value of a man lies in his ability to be useful and be at the service of others. If that character was spread all over the world, there would be less calamities and pacific cohabitation of humanity would no longer be an utopia.

Such example comes from the Lord who said when he became man that he was not here to be served but to serve others.

Mustn't a leader model his conduct to that of the Man-God?

The answer is obvious.

Yes, of course, and his constituents would follow suit, and his country soon would become the model of a peaceful nation—a nation of genuine compatriots lead by a benevolent and selfless leader.

CHAPTER 1

Democracy Against Tyranny Its Benefits and Inconveniences

Throughout history, tyranny has been the enemy of democracy: a form of government defined by etymologists (*demos* means "people" and *kratein* means "govern") as a government of the people, by the people, and for the people.

Such a definition is far from corresponding to reality. It remains an ideal.

The people in its majority don't have the necessary competence to accomplish this noble task. Therefore, the people express their choice through universal suffrage or elections to choose their representatives.

Usually, the people are called during elections, on a day set by the authorities, to put in a box called urn a bulletin in favor of the candidate they choose to endorse as president, senator, deputy, mayor, or other position according to the constitution of the country in question.

Apparently, this is the most acceptable and desired form of government in the world, including the United States of America.

However, it has some disadvantages that must be pointed out, for the people, most of the time, are not able to make the educated or right choice, especially in countries with high rates of political illiteracy.

Usually, the people are unable to determine the most suitable candidate—the one that has the most qualities as a leader.

In order to get there, a candidate would not only have to be well educated, he'll also have to have some political acuity.

By only relying on the submitted program, one should question the candidates on their means to realize their programs, especially in Third World countries where the majority of voters are unable read and write or even tell which candidate is the most suitable for their general well-being, which in reality is something unattainable because politics, in its sacrosanct sense, means the governing of people and things in order to provide the governed with comfort. And the best way to do that is through democracy, which is based on the separation of the three powers of the state known as executive, legislative, and judiciary.

The laws are made by the representatives of the legislative power, deputies, and senators. Most of them sometimes have difficulties defining a law, which is the expression of the people's will. In order to do their job, they must be up to the task. Usually, electoral laws do not require any qualification, legally speaking.

With such shortcomings, they are unable to put together the right legislations in order to advance the state of the country because each power should fulfill its function for a proper functioning of the state, which is defined as a people living freely in a territory.

Sovereignty is indeed delegated to the different powers, among which we have the judiciary system exercised by judges. They can be either elected or appointed by the head of state and approved by the senate. They must make sure the law is applied so that crimes do not remain unpunished and despite great constraints to overcome—namely defendants who think are above the law because of the position they hold, not to mention the threats they receive, personally or to people close to them (husband, wife, children).

Some pessimists say, rightly or wrongly, the law is not human, but divine. Are they right or wrong? You be the judge.

Whatever your answer is, it remains true that the function of a judge is filled with pitfalls and all sorts of traps. However, they must always strive to render justice to whom justice is due. Their role is essential to the well-being of society in order to reach some kind of balance.

However, we are far from perfection, which is fairness before the law. In other words, justice must be meted out in accordance with the crime.

Very often, there are gaps or excesses despite the commitment of politicians to enforce the law. After all, they are human and, as such, are subjects to error like the rest of the common mortals.

They might succumb to substantial bribes or some other offers that can sometimes amount to several years of salary. With that much money involved, they sometimes aren't able to resist the temptation, so they put aside their impartiality to break the law at the expense of the innocents.

Other facts need to be considered here like sometimes the sentencing of a person for years in prison and ultimately find him or her innocent after having serving part or most of their sentence.

Such macabre finding reflects the injustice of the law even though the judge may have acted in good faith. He simply delivered his verdict based on evidences and testimonials so well-orchestrated that they lead to a wrongful conviction.

You can always find reasons to blame the justice system, but the bench holders must do their best to be fair in order to strengthen democracy, which often is unstable.

As for the executive power, the president's role is to make sure the institutions run smoothly. He is responsible of coordinating them without being the center of everything.

Therefore, he should not step on other powers' responsibilities either by refusing to pass a law voted by the congress for instance, or by delaying its passing or by threatening to veto it without real cause to intimidate the legislators in doing their job.

The head of state must work towards the consolidation of democracy in order not to be vulnerable to the opposition's critics. He also must be able to listen to different opinions and, through constructive dialogue, achieve improvements that would be necessary and would benefit the people.

The common goal is security in all areas: alimentation, health, justice, politics, economy.

In a democratic nation, the head of the state is also the first servant alongside senators, congressmen, judges, all elected officials, and civil servants. The law then must be above everyone so no one, no matter your title, should be above of the law. And that is the definition of a state of law.

That way, we will get closer to the ideal world where everyone has a minimum of welfare. We know pure equality is nonexistent, but societies must strive to close the gap between the well-to-do and the less fortunate and between the powerful and the weaker members of society.

In this, it is better to advocate democracy in place of dictatorship. The latter being defined as a form of government in which the head of state has all the powers: executive, legislative, and judicial.

In regard of the fourth power (the press), which is not constitutional, it is muzzled, and the journalists who dare to denounce the abuses of the dictator or monarch disappear without any form of trial. In other words, they are imprisoned, sentenced without trial, or brutally executed, and the other members of the press are forced to be quiet.

Why?

They are attached, like anyone, to their freedoms and life.

We must not believe that under a dictatorial regime, the legislative and judicial powers are inexistent. They are just seen as figurative.

The parliament is just for show, and its role is to endorse the reckless decisions of the executive. It's just a wool over the eyes of the profane to hide the evil face of that form of government that everybody hate but is too afraid to rebel against.

The people are silent so that they avoid the wrath of the regime or its henchmen.

Congressmen and senators come up with bills that are dictated by the executive—often in the form of very well-executed scenarios to distract the people during the voting session. Sometimes, the bill doesn't get enough vote, but somehow, a month later, it comes on the table again. The bill won't necessarily be passed by a large majority. The results would be close as in a parody of a democracy.

Some members of the congress would pretend to protest without any conviction. Those grumblings are buried or postponed indefinitely, never to be heard again. They work for the executive. Sometimes, substantial amendments are made to the main law in order to extend a mandate or to make a reelection possible.

Some even go as far as to declare themselves presidents for life, forgetting that there is only one Eternal—the One who has no beginning and no end.

The head of state controls the congress to the point that the opposition, which should serve as a counter power, is no longer tolerated. Its leaders are persecuted, beaten, or thrown in jail without trial. In cases where there is trial, it's just a show trial where everything is entirely masterminded by the dictator.

The restoration of justice remains a noble cause.

Justice is not fair. So many crimes remain unpunished because the criminals, when they are caught, would go free because of their political connections or threats on the lives of judges and their families.

Every time there is chaos on the streets, it's because of former offenders who had been reintegrated to society by the executive, extending his reach on all parts of the society that blindly obey.

Such a way of governing defies common sense and sows terror among the population. If they show any sign of revolt or disagreement, they are immediately apprehended by the police who, normally, should be the auxiliary of the justice system but, in reality, is under the control of the executive. The latter has absolute and unwavering powers.

In order to preserve its omnipotence, any kind of fragmentation of its authority is banned.

However, what the tyrant forgets is the impossibility to last, because longevity doesn't mix well with dictatorship.

Often, it's of short duration, and when there is an uprising, it's complete chaos, with the unrepentant leader completely lost and disillusioned being degraded by the people. He's then not even half of the man he used to be. If he doesn't end up condemned with the utmost rigor, he would be dragged from place to place, his body ripped apart by an angry mob.

He ought to be moderate and tolerant and not be extreme, which can lead to the people's dissatisfaction.

Truth be told, we must admit that though one can keep the people under dictatorship for a while, they cannot be silenced forever.

Our hero made the wrong choice when he chose to be a dictator. That will lead to his demise, just like all the leaders who chose brutal force as a way of governing.

The people would feel frustrated with the whole system. In order to avoid being impeached, he would make bad decisions after bad decisions—all that because he thinks he is the center of the universe.

Such philosophy tends to poison good governance, and sooner or later, it's going to be a debacle. So why does our hero think he can identify himself with power?

He's going to surely regret acting outside the norms. If he conformed to the rules, he would have avoided so many problems both to him and his country. Maybe he was the victim of the mania of power concentration.

He risked his life being so reckless and missed an opportunity to do great things. Everyone who is in a position of power must be at the service of the people and allow them to live decent lives.

The biggest dictators are also the least of the servants. The King of all kings didn't hesitate to lower himself in order to serve and save humanity.

CHAPTER 2

Portrait of Governor John Redlight

Elected governor of a southern state in the United States in his late twenties, he was physically well-built and had a lot of charisma.

He looked more like a rock star than a politician. Wherever he went, women of all ages would cheer him, and his security detail were composed mainly of a group of beautiful young women with dark glasses, like the security detail of a certain colonel from a North African country.

When his popularity reached its peak, he decided to run for president of the United States of America. When they watched him, the ladies would be completely charmed. Some of them preferred to ogle at him to better contemplate his body.

"A pure gem, fallen from the hands of God," some of his admirers would say. Others would rather be silent and admire his whole body, which was masterfully cut by the Creator. His slender figure would provoke goose bumps to women. Quite often, when addressing his constituents, people were more interested in his posture than in what he was saying.

Many young socialites dreamed awake or asleep about meeting him alone to talk to him for even seconds. The leader, too, would love to be alone with them, but his job prevented him from satisfying those needs.

He had a passion for sweet adventures—imagining himself with all kinds of ladies and paying no mind to his condition. Every woman, to him, was a prey that if he cannot devour the flesh, he would smell the perfume.

He used to say that if the world of women was so beautiful, it was to better serve men, and even though they are the weaker sex, they are able to completely destroy a man and reduce him to his simplest expression.

Fortunately, the governor was an exception to this rule. It was women who quietly desired to catch him in their nets. Such an idea cannot correspond to reality.

They often were too taciturn to hide their feelings towards that beautiful ladies man. He, too, deep inside, wanted to dance with them, but unfortunately, his position prevented him to join them since a governor is not free to move however he wants. He was protected by his bodyguards who, maybe, should have helped him get with his prettiest admirers.

However, he could not see himself making such a deal with his bodyguards. They would have been reprimanded for allowing such dangerous behavior.

These considerations prove, if proof were needed, the responsibilities linked to such profession. Was it necessary to condemn him still?

He was human; therefore, he cannot be blamed for it. Just because he was chasing tails, blaming him for that would have been against human nature.

Was it reasonable to hang him for his inclinations? Not at all.

Everyone has their flaws, and given that he had outstanding physical qualities, his path was singular: not as a leader, but more as womanizer, to the point that some people thought he would far e better as a model and that all the clothes he would wear would be sold in auctions to the highest bidder.

He was sculpted by the hands of a great artist from another world. Therefore, any partner, lover, or wife would have a hard time containing their jealousy even though he had no intention of flirting with the thousands of women that wish to have a taste of a person so radiant at least once in their lives.

So he was envied all over the world. Let's get closer in order to better describe him without missing a detail. "He shines a thousand lights. He is a handsome man!" exclaimed one of his admirers once.

Another one interrupted her, "It wasn't even a fraction of the truth concerning that man who differed from other men to a point never equaled. More than a handsome man, he's an angel. Therefore, he belongs to the divine and walks among humans. His element should be the highest of heavens, close to God."

"If that was the case, we would not have the chance to see him with our eyes of the body or even that of the soul."

"When you look at him, you can see many facets of his beauty"

"You're right"

"Sometimes, his body lets out the seven colors of the rainbow."

"If that's true, he's a privileged man who uses his charms to help the needy."

"You're really fascinated by him."

"I cannot help it?"

"Unless you're blind, and even then, your other senses would sense his miraculous light."

"That's right."

"He's a perfect product."

"A product of whom?"

"A product of nature, but with a touch of something unknown to other human beings."

"You're a real poet, you know that."

"I became one after seeing his beautiful smile."

"You are lucky you saw him smiling. Whoever saw his smile can consider themselves very fortunate."

"There are people who are so lucky, they should thank the Lord for having made our governor so special."

"If he dared to venture in other places, he would probably get kidnapped by some lady. She would keep him to herself and cherish him in a secret place, not to torture him but to make him her private property."

"He would then need a lot of energy to satisfy the needs of that lucky woman, who would require his favors day and night."

"She would be satisfied."

"Not at all, because such sweetness can only be beneficial with moderation. You might get addicted to the point you won't be able to do anything else."

"You have a really fertile imagination."

"More than that, I fantasize presently for such delightful future."

"Indeed, he is tall, charming, and muscular. He had blond hair like gold that delicately fell to his square shoulders. His face was shaped beautifully and gently lit by his complexion in a way that he looked like an angel. His two, big blue eyes were so bright that they looked like rubies. His nose was perfectly shaped, long and thin, and incomparable. His delicate lips were made to give young flowers unforgettable kisses. His teeth were extremely white.

"He seemed just perfect, immaculate, spotless, at first sight, but he struggled to fight the temptation of so many temptresses, even though he would succumb to some of them one way or another.

"The truth is, even by multiplying his capacities until the end of his life, he would not be able to satisfy some of them, let it be the prettiest that can compete with Venus, the goddess of beauty.

"Many women would love to have a memory of one of his indiscretions. They would have been more than flattered to have a taste of his heavenly honey. Every woman, even the queens and empresses, would love to have him as a companion of road, table, or bed.

"It would be necessary, while he was alive, to immortalize him by having everywhere around the city, statues of him for people to honor him and not wait his death to start really appreciate him. Moreover, even before his death, the women of his generation and beyond thanked him for being a model of the art in which is shaped the human being.

"He was one of a kind. Having him as husband would probably be great joy, even though his wife would be expected to suffer from jealousy even in her dreams. She showed her jealousy in public in a manner that's deemed unbecoming of the wife of a governor of that caliber and even less of that of a president of the biggest economic and military power of the world, the United States of America.

"A First Lady who has a hard time with tendentious looks and glances from young girls, women, and even teenagers toward her husband would need a lot of strength not to burst into tears since the protocol was opposed to such displays.

"She needed lots of self-control, a daunting and unbearable task. It would have been OK if it was in private, where they could talk about it, but in public.

"They were equals then. Neither of them had a superior status. They needed to act like two love birds with the same rights and forming a single body without any kind of hierarchy.

"In addition to his inherent qualities, the fluid that emanated from his physical charms fascinated many, if not everyone. If, fortunately, he ever smiled at you, you would be hanging to each of his words, hypnotized by his lips. Besides, he never shows a sinister face. He spreads joy. When he turned, the silhouette of his whole body showed limitless elegance.

"His walk could hypnotize you, having you follow him with your eyes to the point where he would disappear, leaving you completely baffled. You would then wish to meet him again to look at him walk again. One could then wonder how lucky his wife was.

"It's maybe a bitter happiness that led her to want to keep him prisoner, in vain.

"That's why the joy didn't even last a day. He was like lightning, ephemeral to the eyes of others. He shined permanently and could be compared to none of his ascendants or collaterals. How did he become so special?

"The answer is obvious. From the one who makes impossible things possible, since what is extraordinary to humans is ordinary to the Lord. He had exceptional and mysterious qualities.

"Due to our limited intelligence, we cannot explain with details how someone can be so beautiful made."

CHAPTER 3

His Run for Presidency

His beauty was the major asset for his campaign.

He resigned as governor to run for president. To get elected, he needed to beat more than seven candidates during the primaries. He managed to succeed with the help of the media and the female vote. He easily became the leading candidate of the general elections.

He ran against a Republican and an independent candidate. In order to reach his goals, he relied on his most valuable asset: his physical attraction and the free publicity of the media.

No one could defeat him. As for the feminine electorate, they showed absolute loyalty to him.

It was more than certain that the majority of them, more than men, would fight to get him to the White House so they could contemplate his body, even if it's through a TV set.

This led to heated discussions all around the country, on the Internet, on social media, between husbands and wives, between women of all ages: teenagers, young adults, middle-aged women, and even old ladies.

They dreamed to see him close in order to, later, fall into his arms. They would then feel more than happy to flirt with that rare specimen of a man.

No one could remain indifferent to him. Even the husbands, though filled with jealousy, were ready to endorse his candidacy.

Were they right to do so? It was completely foolish of them, if you ask me, because the candidate is not a stallion. Even by multiplying his energy, he would not be able to satisfy even a portion of this female parade. Their level of jealousy exceeded all limits.

The husbands could not blame their wives since they have cheated on them so many occasions in the past. Even though they were unfaithful, they strongly wished their wives to remain faithful and not sin even in their heart by lusting over the sample of humanity in their soul and in their mind.

The women did not covet his body. They were conscious that they would never be fortunate enough. The candidate was and remained a wonder, a phenomenon.

It was impossible for that precious governor to lose the race for the White House. His favorite weapon was his beauty, which played in his favor beyond reason, and no other candidate, may they be Republican or Democrat, could stop him.

When God favors you, no one, regardless of their status, can mess up His will. Especially since it is said, according to the Christian conception of power, that it comes from above.

It looked like he was predestined since the dawn of eternity to become a leader of the most powerful country on earth. He was extremely blessed, for he was made with more dexterity than the other privileged men. He was one of a kind.

Did he deserve all these divine gifts? Not at all, but God wished him to get all these advantages and resources. Physically, he seemed simply perfect, and everyone was ready to support him in his noble quest without even questioning his political projects.

Most people thought deep inside that if the candidate is blessed with such attractive body, God would also bless him with wonderful ideas and the means to realize them.

He was totally trusted even before he presented his political program and provided us with the details on how he was going to implement his policies.

If you ask me, that was very childish of the voters. But that's what the people wanted. Trying to open their eyes would have been a waste of time; you would be met with jokes and sarcasms.

Therefore, it was extremely rare to find people who didn't take part of that frenzy of total support at various points.

Wouldn't they better call him "the miracle candidate"?

The many doors that separated him from his goal started opening one after another. People were then drawn in the fever of the passion around this man who from the start was considered a messiah sent to provide welfare to everyone in America.

There was no reason to compete with him. It would have been a lost cause. You would have been constantly mocked for that before being buried alive.

There are those who are gifted and bound to succeed. Don't try to find a reason for that because even if there are some, only reason can detect them. It's the least we can say.

It's wrong to try and contradict what's reasonable by nature. It's like trying to dry the ocean. However, we could wonder where to find the empty spaces to lead this avalanche.

The truth compels us to admit that the entire campaign of trying to compete with him was in vain because they just had no chance.

Some people said it was written in eternity that no one could stand in his way. More than trust, people had complete faith in him.

Indeed, at the announcement of the date and place or specifically when the time and duration determined for a rally, hotels were booked solid in town by an exceptional staff at the image of the candidate.

Hotels were overbooked with reservations. No one wanted to miss the opportunity to take close-up pictures of the candidate with the most sophisticated cameras.

The residents of the city, weeks in advance, had asked for leave of absence that day, and there were so many requests that some companies decided to close that day to avoid pissing off their employees.

When they learned of the news, employees were ecstatic. They thanked their bosses publicly on the radio and on TV. The people's excitement spread all over town to the point that the mayor decided to give the day off to all city employees, since they would not show to work anyway. His decision was highly appreciated by the workers but annoyed certain people in the community and the opposite camp.

Some individuals, the day before his arrival, impulsively started decorating the roads that the convoy was going to drive on. Unbelievable, yet true!

For more than a week, outsiders rushed to the town. The coffee shops were crowded, restaurants were filled with clients, and the bars were packed. People wanted the privilege to meet the future hero.

Beside his good looks, he was also a sweet talker. He was a master of communication, so it was not difficult for him to easily convince his audience even though much of his talk was more demagoguery than substance. He was able to galvanize crowds with his sweet words. His strategy was to charm women by using peremptory arguments and persuade people to massively vote for him.

He didn't even need to convince people. He had all the cards, all the resources; there were no doubt he was going to win. Still, he showed nothing but humility.

He could not act otherwise because boasting is a sign of weakness.

His humility was a bonus to better capture people's attention and to get the most favorable votes—to the point that everyone wondered if he needed that much advantages.

He was meticulous in his choices of clothes and words. Before any public appearance, he made sure he spent time with a couple of handpicked makeup artists.

They would offer their services for free and made sure they use all their talents to perform their task, trying to add special notes in the execution of the work, especially regarding his foundation.

They took advantage of the situation to gently caress his face, making sure they didn't arouse any suspicion about their hidden agendas.

If they were caught, they risk being banned from the profession. In other words, they would lose their license for lusting over male beauties.

As professionals, they acted with caution and avoided excess. They restrained themselves in order to contain their passions.

This unique being had the difficult choice to accept or reject these exciting offers. More than lucky, he was fortunate.

He benefited from a favorable destiny and was particularly gifted. In reality, fortune should designate God, not a man, but he was in a way godly. He had many virtues. People didn't even see him to be attracted to his star power. His angelic voice spoke sentences with words that were not only well-organized, but also excellently structured.

No audience could resist his flamboyant verve, speaking perfectly his thoughts. He was made to seduce either with his physique or with his words as dictated by providence.

Inspiration came directly to him from the beyond. No one could believe their own eyes and ears. It was not rare for a woman after she attended a meeting of his to find her husband in a bad mood.

"Honey, why the long face? Didn't I tell you I was going to the meeting of the candidate that has no rivals for the upcoming presidential elections?"

"Yes, I knew, but next time, please don't tell me about it."

"But why? Do you think I would cheat on you because you're not as privilege as he is? Do you doubt my loyalty?"

"Let's be serious. No woman could resist the charms of the candidate."

"It's disrespect to me. He's a hero."

"You understand why I am not happy? Compared to your hero, no man could claim to be able to keep his woman. Not to mention that she would feel honored with even a look from that extraterrestrial man."

"You found the right word. However, that term only gives us a virtual image of that exceptional being, made to shine. He is brilliant, he radiates. When you see him, you get goose bumps."

"That's the naked truth. Honey, you're so sincere! Do you promise me you'll always stay attached to me?"

"Of course."

"Why didn't you answer maybe instead? Only if you are not pursued by that bright star."

"Enough. Stop insulting me."

"I'm not. . . just kidding."

The chosen one provoked such fever that people in every town and village went to vote for him. Were they fans?

Such expression of love could only be destined to a human being of this caliber.

After a few meetings far from the heart of the electoral campaign, he received so many tempting offers from almost every American city formulated by both the mayors and hundreds of thousands of zealous supporters.

They were excited to meet him. His rallies also were good for business. It was a total consecration before election day.

His campaign receptionists were swamped with phone calls of people offering their credit card numbers to donate substantial amount of money to the campaign. People he had never met, who were attracted by his silhouette they saw on TV or social media, were donating.

Some city leaders had to lobby, hoping that their towns would be on the list of cities visited by the candidate.

Their role was to provide the campaign officials with the people's demands. Within three days, they raised an unbelievable amount of funds: more than ninety million dollars.

Marathons and fund-raisers were organized in every town. Even children would bring their meager contribution after they were charmed, not to mention the contribution of teenagers, adults, and old people.

On the fourth day, more than seventy million was added to the contributions. It was insane!

Some car companies offered free vehicles to the campaign, hoping that one of their models would be part of the convoy. For them, that would be great advertisement. That's why lobbyists voted for him so that they could do good business.

People were campaigning to take advantage of the campaign. Everyone felt honored on election day to cast a ballot for the adored candidate.

Every other country in the world wished one day they had such candidate—someone who would drastically change the destiny of their country in a positive way, not in a bad way.

They strongly believed that the Unites States of America were favored in more ways than one. They were the leading economic, military, and scientific power, and they also had this enviable person that is the world's star.

Needless to say his name, better not say anything. The American people who went to vote for him knew his first and last name; they even knew the name of his ancestors. He did not yet have any offspring.

Women wished his first child would be a boy to extend the line with distinction. People liked to consider him as an art—nectar that covers the morning star with its sweet aroma.

His admirers were exaggerating, but they could not be blamed for their commitment. They had every reason to worship such a flawless personality.

At that rate, without any exaggeration, journalists from all sides wanted one day to interview him, even for ten minutes.

They knew they would become more famous after interviewing him and the ratings along would bring millions to their respective media outlet...

Talking to him face to face and being around him was more precious than winning the lottery to some. Honor is better than money because money cannot buy honor, some will declare. It was a total frenzy. People were captivated in an incomparable way. It's the least we can say.

From east to west, north to south, from the arctic region to the temperate zone of the northern hemisphere, to the inhabited lands of Antarctica, there was one face to look at, one speech to listen to religiously, and they belonged to the miracle one.

Everyone thought he was loved and venerated, if not adored. That would be too much. Everyone agreed in recognizing the truth of the passion caused by this outstanding candidate.

In reality, he was cheered by supporters of all traditional parties. A revolution was taking place in the country.

He was considered a creature from another dimension unknown to us. He was a complete mystery.

As election day approached, the security barriers made approaching him increasingly more difficult. They had to build him a bulletproof glass cage. Nevertheless, we could hear thunderous applauses around him.

To control and contain the crowd, he didn't need to talk or detail his program. His fans said the future president was a model not only for the United States but for the entire world.

Such immoderate reflections could be read all over the press, which caused a lot of headaches to the current head of states in the United States and all over the world.

He could then, without a doubt, consider himself the winner well before election day.

Finally, the long awaited day came in the United States. You could see enthusiasm in the face of the people. It was like he ran unopposed.

It was a landslide. He won 90 percent of the votes with an unbelievable participation rate: 80 percent of people in age to vote. A real consecration.

It was meant to be that way. The night of the elections he appeared on TV in a packed stadium filled to capacity, with people throughout the world listening and watching, to announce his victory. Maybe triumph would have been a better characterization.

Dressed in a dark-gray suit, his face shone a thousand lights when he said, "First of all, let me thank God for leading me to this position of responsibility. I could not have imagined, in my life, being the winner today. I want to thank the American people of all confessions, of all ideologies. I'm victorious today because of a divine gift and the unconditional trust of millions of my fellow Americans.

"My fellow Americans, words fail me to express my deep gratitude toward your unfading support., This victory is not my victory but yours, since this day could not be possible without this tidal wave of fans and supporters. Let us work together to make this dream a reality, to make America great again for all its children. I've received a call from my opponent to congratulate me and several head of States have already sent their message of congratulations. Let us put ourselves to work from now on to rebuilt this great country that is the envy of the world. I pledge to do my utmost not to disappoint you. May God bless you and may he blessed the United States of America"

A thunderous applause followed that lasted over five minutes.

" "

His rise to power was crowned by his inauguration. It was an unprecedented event. His inauguration was a first in the history of this country. The budget for the festivities was so huge that the entire country was having a big party to celebrate the elections of this one of a kind politician.

He was a radiant prodigy that amazes in his singularity. Some people were skeptical. They wondered how this was possible. They forgot that nothing is impossible to a genius. He was able to make possible what seems impossible.

The chosen one had undoubtedly benefited from an amazing favor. Still, he was questioning why he was receiving that much blessings.

He felt the duty not to disappoint the voters, the people who elected him president with an overwhelming majority.

In private, he said that the euphoria after the victory was short-lived. Without waiting, he would have to work hard with his team to try and better the lives of as many people as possible. That is to say, not only the *primum vivere*, but also allow everyone to enjoy the basic of this great nation without which people would undoubtedly fall into poverty.

The Actual Inaugural Ceremony

Representatives of almost every country in the world attended the ceremony. It was an honor for them to be invited to this historical event and to shake hands with this titanic hero.

Among the prominent guests were: the queen of England and the prime minister, the French president, the German chancellor, the prime minister of Canada, the kings of Belgium and Spain, several sheiks and kings from the Middle East, even the pope attended. There were many more; naming them all would be an endless task.

After taking the customary oath on the Bible and declaring he would respect the Constitution of the country and the democratic traditions, he pronounced his solemn speech:

"His Holiness, the pope, Her Majesty, the queen, royalties from different kingdoms, presidents, prime ministers, honorable members of the diplomatic corps, honorable members of the United States Congress, honorable judges of the Supreme Court, fellow citizens.

"In this blessed day, I want to start by thanking the Almighty who put me in this position of president of the United States of America.

"My undeniable popularity is God's eternal wish according to the charismatic conception of power, which advocates that power comes from above, that is to say, from the Almighty.

"May his name be glorified, and may his laudatory epithets be blessed, mainly on this day. God bless America, and may we keep believing in him, with our faith, our hopes and dreams of better days.

"Thanks to him, I became president of the world's leading power. He gave me a major advantage, which is the ability to amaze people with my physique, combined with a flamboyant verve allowing me to handle words with angelic dexterity.

"In other words, speeches take form in me, of course figuratively, in order to galvanize the crowds to vote for me.

"It was a total storm, not to lead you towards an abyss, but to allow me to be alert and smart enough to manage the assets of the state and provide well-being to everyone.

"Let the wealthy consent not to sacrifice their wealth, but to share a tiny part of their surplus so that the majority would benefit from a minimum of wealth. That way, they would become, with time, even before the end of my term, a bit wealthier alongside the rich, the richer, the very rich or super rich. That way, we could bribe their frustration, and the economically powerful will continue to have fun in their overabundance.

"This way, we would bring together the two worlds of the poor and rich, at least in America, and I'm sure the rest of the world would follow this blueprint.

"May the prosperity of the minority cease to lie on the poverty of the majority!

"Also, if the workers become less poor, they would work harder for the benefit of the corporations... That would lead to even greater benefits and better salaries. The employees would enjoy basic human rights. . . balanced food ratio, drinkable water, decent housing, health care when they are sick, a good education. . .

"Let's make that dream a reality right now, thanks to God. May he make possible what seems impossible. I ask the Lord to help me be wise enough to become the servant of my constituents, in close collaboration with the other two powers, legislative and judicial.

"May we all work together to make America remain the world's leading power, collaborating with the rest of the world, not to exploit them but to help end poverty and wars so that peace would reign on the seven continents. In order words I want to make America great again.

"In our will to fraternize with the rest of the world, the emphasis will be put on economic progress.

"May Providence grant us prosperity, not just for our country, but for the entire world and lead us towards a new era of universal elevation in all areas. Everything is possible to mankind with the help of the universal providence. Let it be known to the world that America will remain its leader to provide stability and world peace. Let the agents of terror know that their time is up, for my government will be relentless in the fight against the scourge of terrorism. God bless the United States of America, and may His blessings be on the American people."

CHAPTER 4

Sad Face of the First Lady
During the Inauguration

What astonished the guests, spectators, and viewers all over the world was the sad face of the First Lady standing next to her husband.

On more than one occasion, she seemed to be crying. Thank goodness she refrained herself from bitterly sobbing in public. Her attitude was attributed to the intensity of her joy.

If that was the case, they would have been tears of joy because according to the old saying, "When joy crosses the threshold of glee to peak toward jubilation, tears would appear under the effect of an internal cause." Here, her jealousy, or more precisely, her burning desire was to totally possess him and subtract him from the lusty gazes of other women.

However, she knew her husband's passion for women already when he was governor, and now that he is president, she believed that he will be uncontrollable .

The fights became more and more intense as she would keep spying on him during his multiple travels, when he would take refuge in the Oval Office to receive visitors and employees, or during his phone conversation—trying to find out what he is up to, especially since her husband was an expert in hiding things from her.

While he was beloved as a head of state, to her, the most important thing was her husband. She could have deprived him of herself in order to dominate him. But such strategy would have failed since he had other choices—indeed, other women, some true jewels and way better looking than her who would be more than happy to substitute in her place.

She loved her husband with passion, but he didn't love her in return. He was an expert in new love affairs. Fortunately for him, his staff and other employees didn't detect that flaw in him.

It was better for them to ignore the president's tendencies in that area. Such information could have cost him the presidency, and that would have been bad for the First Lady too who would lose her position.

Thanks to her flair, she noticed that the women in his staff were beauties able to catch any man's attention, especially her husband's.

Inside, she wondered if it would be better for her husband not to become president, though she enjoyed being First Lady.

However, she knew she would not be able to enjoy the perks attached to the position of First Lady. She understood she had to be extremely vigilant even though that wouldn't help since she could not enter the Oval Office when the president is in audience.

In reality, she is so stressed that she would get completely frigid at night in the marital bed due to her doubts on the fidelities of her husband in that area.

Over time, she found out he had a special relationship with one beautiful creature on his staff. She was a rival to Venus, perfectly built, and matching in beauty with her husband.

Ironically, she didn't think anything of all the endless conversations between the two to the point that it woke the suspicion of some employees who started whispering among themselves about the reason for that situation.

They did not dare say anything about it, but some made a big deal out of it.

"The First Lady doesn't really fit the president."

"What do you mean?"

"She's not very pretty."

"She has to dress a certain way, according to protocol."

"Indeed, her naked sleeves don't fit protocol."

"She wishes to be hip to catch attention?"

"Do you think she might be unfaithful?"

"No one would dare thinking so."

"Because her husband is a star, she might be tempted to compete with him."

"You're exaggerating."

"But the president doesn't care."

"Up to this point."

"He would feel freed."

"He's embarrassed by her."

"How come?"

"People wonder if it wouldn't be better for her to just go away."

"That would be the biggest scandal to ever happen at the White House."

"According to the maid, The First Lady sleeps in a separate room."

"That's a rumor."

"Some women, if not most, are indiscreet."

"They look for confidantes then turn them into so-called secrets."

"That's right. There is no secret between two persons or more."

"There's a rumor I don't know if it's true or not, but they say that the president meets privately twice or three times a day with a female employee at times when he doesn't meet with staff, and it's always the same woman, to the point that her superiors would reprimand her out of jealousy."

"Who is she?"

"It's Miss beautiful, that's what they call her."

"She's really elegant."

"In that field, the president has good taste."

"But maybe they just meet to talk about businesses about the section or he wanted to ask for advice."

"She's not the one in charge. He would rather have to talk to the chief of staff, Mister Henry Williams."

"In any case, he has his favorites."

"That's too bad!"

"Such disparaging rumors!"

"About what?"

"About intimate relations."

"Impossible, in the Oval Office!"

"Aren't there surveillance cameras in there?"

"Sure, to ensure the safety of the president."

"Naturally. If that's the case, let's come back one day during the holidays to watch the tapes and look for any kind of shenanigans."

"That would be the first thing to soil the image of our hero."

"Such a man, so fond of women. . ."

"If the rumors are true, the First Lady is right to be on the edge. She's not about to forgive him."

"She defends her interests."

"But she could share him with other women."

"These kinds of rumors tend to spread like wildfire whether they're true or not."

"It's not bad news."

"On the contrary, people would be delighted by that news."

"To some extent, I agree with you. What's the point of being selfish when we want to be with more than one person?"

"Sharing joy, far from diminishing it, can lead to more elevated life than dividing joy."

"A fallacy, outside of the most basic sense of morality."

"All that is dictated by love is sacrosanct."

"You'd make a great lawyer."

"I am one, though I don't work in that capacity in the White House."

"This suggests that the wife and the lover of the president are not to blame."

"Blaming them would be total injustice. The fruits of love, especially erotic fruits, are always juicy even when they cause the dismay of the people involved."

"What a theory!"

"It should be rejected right away."

"Not so quick, because it's nature. No human being can generate both."

"It would be better to try and control one's natural urges in such troubling times."

"Because it's about the love of a president for one of his staff members."

"He is a human being, like everyone else. So nothing human can be alien to him."

"But he lacks restraint."

"In your opinion, he should hold his impulses back?"

"Why not?"

"And, in that case, for how long?"

"During his term."

"For four years."

"Over the years, his soul and spirit would be so crushed to oblivion."

"But he could wait a few months."

"For what?"

"He's only beating the iron while it's still hot."

"He caught the ball."

"Could he find a way to escape this?"

"Unless there comes a time when he is attracted to another. . ."

"This makes things worse. Might there be three women fighting for a piece of him?"

"You mean a piece of the *prey*."

"We'll have to wait and see the impact of this in the palace."

"We can expect the worse in the coming days."

"Let's wait and see."

"Do you think this time bomb would shake the White House over?"

"It might shake the whole country over."

"If you're right, the consequences might be catastrophic."

"For the United States of America, but not for the rest of the world."

"You ignore that the US is the world's leading power, militarily, economically, and scientifically. Each year, there is at least one American winning a Nobel Prize in a given field. Therefore, any kind of rumble in the White house, any flu of the US, can result in tuberculosis everywhere else."

"For those reasons, our leader should control his carnal appetites."

"No one would dare to say anything to him because these scenes happen in private."

"But he doesn't know that his intimacy could be made the business of everyone."

"I fear he would have to resign due to a socially unacceptable act."

"He's the first citizen of the country. His behavior should be exemplary."

"Fortunately, he's not getting carried away by his animal instincts but his feelings of love."

"If ever they learn about the offenses of their leader, wouldn't the people be right to be scandalized?"

"And no one can predict the consequences on his government."

"If that was confirmed and proved, he would face countless troubles."

"He could get impeached for this."

"It's that serious."

"It's considered a crime, adultery without mitigation.

"Do you think it's possible to prosecute him?"

"Of course."

"In any case, I wish this dirty laundry to be washed in the presidential house."

"It's impossible. Journalists love these kinds of sensational news."

"There is a way of alerting the media. They are willing to go any length just to have a piece of the news."

"This is our chance to become millionaires, if we sell this story."

"But we might get removed if the leak is revealed after some time."

In that case, it would be wise to remain silent and keep working for our meager wages because if things go wrong, we would lose our jobs."

Out of this dialogue appeared the hypothesis of repercussions able to completely dismantle the system since the lovesick man in charge could make unexpected decisions to remain in power. He might try to ignore the democratic principles that the country is built on. Even though he was considered as a model of righteousness, his image of perfect man will be tarnished later.

We could fear that the wave that got him in power would turn against him to completely annihilate him and rightfully push him out of the White House.

It would be an abominable crime that would force him to resign. That could be prosecuted before the court. This is quite a pessimist view, but it's a possibility.

It's a shame that might happen to such a leader. It's unbelievable, really! In any case, if such a crime is not punished, his dozens of millions fans would be greatly disappointed when they would learn about it.

Nothing and no one will be able to contain the people's disappointment and sorrow. They would be ready to hold him accountable for his ignominious behavior.

They would even wish him to be sentenced to life imprisonment to prevent the next presidents from acting like Don Juan, and encourage them to be moderate leaders who respect basic conventions like being faithful to their wives and not cheat on them, at least during their mandate.

The president has to conform to the principles of fidelity in marriage, especially since he is the leader of the nation.

For succumbing to temptation, he should consider himself guilty and recognize his faults, though they would plunge him into a whirlwind of disgrace.

CHAPTER 5

Tense Relations Between the
White House and the Congress

The extramarital relations of the president created a weird atmosphere among the White House employees. There were backstage whispers about his affair.

There were many discussions about the president. He reacted quite nonchalantly, thinking he could save face.

While Congress and the White House were bumping heads about the budget, the people's representatives chose not to approve the budget for the current fiscal year. This caused the closure of most public offices due to default of salary payment.

Even the White House was forced to get rid of its nonessential staff, and in order to preserve her identity, the president decided to fire the woman whom he had an affair with.

At this stage, he was more concerned with his sexual indiscretions than the public welfare, especially since he knew most of the Congress was aware of his moral dilemmas.

To fill the empty positions in the White House, they hired some young interns. Among the newcomers, a beautiful girl and a real star, caught the attention of the president, a complete impenitent lover.

She got his heart beating fast. She was then invited to the Oval Office. She found her host sad and melancholic.

He seemed stressed and tortured. He seemed worried about his unbridled behavior. Nevertheless, he was ready to reactivate for that goddess.

"Sit down," the president told her, completely charmed by the slender figure of the beautiful woman with the unique eyes.

In front of beautiful women, he would be a simple valet. It's a complete contradiction to see a world leader be so subordinate to a woman.

She was surprised by the sweet and melancholic tone of the president's voice when he invited her to sit. She never expected to be greeted with such kindness. She could neither believe her eyes nor her ears. She felt such honor could disconcert her. Therefore, she got ready to take complete advantage of a lover who is incapable of self-control.

That's a really derogatory way to describe a president! He suffered from lovesickness that got him helpless in front of a woman. In no time, she managed to detect the degree of submission of the powerful man.

"Why are you so sad?" she asked.

"I'm lovesick. I have a bone to pick with my wife."

"You probably neglected her. You have so many responsibilities. She feels neglected. How does she react? Don't tell me that she cut you off?"

"You're absolutely right. She decided to sleep in a separate room. All that because some unfounded rumors she heard around. She blames me for having publicly humiliated her. Some people call me crazy in love. . . no, not to my face. I heard that by proxy."

"If she's acting that way, it's because you displeased her somehow. Maybe you gave her a rival who's way prettier than her."

"Not really."

"She's not crazy. Her jealousy is based on something real."

"Still, she should stand next to me, especially since my relationship with that woman was purely platonic."

"Were you able to control yourself? Could you separate friendship from love? If you ask me, love always starts with friendship. You don't need be a psychologist to know that."

Very quickly, a line was crossed, and that's no one's fault. According to the old saying: "The spirit is willing, but the flesh is weak."

"To be honest, I must confess that I feel very alone. I have no one to talk to. Would you help me with that?"

"I would not. I don't know what I could do to make you smile again. In any case, don't count on me."

When he heard those words, the president (sorry, Mister Lover) started sobbing so much that the walls shook. He was weeping bitterly.

"I'm finished. I want to die, once and for all! My life has no purpose. I want God to take my unbearable life. What have I done to deserve this? I'm done. I don't care anymore. I'm hopeless."

When she heard his disconcerting cries of despair, she felt touched in the bottom of her heart. She then got closer to the president to console him and said, "Don't worry, I'm here."

From then on, she started gently touching his face, then his shoulder. The lucky man immediately stopped crying.

She moved her gentle hands back to his face, caressing it. The president's whole body and soul began to shiver—this time with joy. Now they are holding hands, looking at each other's eyes. Then a first wet kiss that would probably be followed by a thousand others. There was mutual chill mixed with sensual and rhythmical sighs.

They hugged increasingly stronger and embraced each other.

The sighs got more intense. Their clothes were off in no time. Completely naked, there was no way of telling them apart.

For a short moment, they were one unique body—and all this, in the middle of the Oval Office.

It was the beginning of a love story that was destined to last.

For how long? No one knew, and the two lovers could not know what the future would hold. Only God has that power. That was a rebirth for the president who just met the woman of his dreams.

How lucky he was!

He needed nothing then, but no one knew what was coming next. All his desires were fulfilled. He was so enamored with that goddess that he was willing to put her above himself.

By any means, he wished to keep her near, against all odds. He was convinced that love prevailed over politics. He didn't see the danger in that, though by embarking on that path, he possibly risked losing his presidency. Apparently, he didn't care one bit.

He was primarily concerned with beautiful and caring women. He was focused on one idea. In reality, he was a fool to fall for such illusions. He was too extreme, consequently, he suffered imbalance since he was not moderate.

However, this time, he hoped his relationship would remain unknown to the general public. That was wrong, childish, and naive of him. That's the least we could say.

He was unable to be without his new conquest and was even willing to meet with her outside the White House.

He was filled with passion. Some would even say that he became the definition of passion.

As for her, she was also under his charm. She realized how lucky she was to be the lover of the president of the United States—the leader of the greatest military, economic, and scientific power in the world. She even dreamt of one day becoming First Lady.

Why not?

She even tried to ask her lover to divorce his wife. She was ambitious, but why not? She is a woman.

Often, the two stars' behavior would betray the strong ties they had.

Such situation and ambition were too important to remain in hiding. Asking for confidentiality was then impossible.

It would have been possible if they were in a relationship that complied with social standards—in other words, if they were married.

They were foolish to believe otherwise.

For the president, this was adultery; for the temptress, this was fornication.

Despite everything, we could still hope for a miracle. Given that he had always been lucky, he kept being delusional since until then, his affairs remained private.

Why not? But the mistress considered her situation as a miracle. She saw herself fit to confide in her mother and one envious colleague of hers.

So much honor, being the president's lover that is, could not remain hidden.

Her confidence was recorded without her knowing. The tapes were then sent to the head of the opposition party. This was a great opportunity to discredit his rival.

Usually in politics, the opposition is the archnemesis of the regime in power. In reality, there might have been some meetings in order to take the necessary steps to correct certain errors for the public good.

This was not the way people should act to protect the nation's interests. They mainly wanted a way to prevent the person in power to finish his mandate.

It's true when they say that politics is not the science of saints. It maybe the demon's.

You be the judge.

CHAPTER 6

Talks to Impeach the President

The president continued his reckless and sweet meetings with the woman he loves without worrying about what people were saying. He was swimming in happiness and neglected the major interests of the nation.

He was being outrageously selfish! For him, the important thing was his carnal pleasure. A real fairy tale! He wanted more meetings, haunted by the idea of making his lover the First Lady.

He exaggerates most people would say, ignoring the power of erotic love over anything else.

Maybe they forgot about the European monarch who chose to abdicate the throne to marry the woman of his dreams.

On the contrary, he felt he didn't have enough time for his lover. He neglected everything around him. Only one being was in his mind. He didn't care one bit about the good governance of men and things. Instead he only cared about maintaining his love life, making sure he did everything he could to please his beautiful jewel made by the hands of God.

The intermittent companion was more than enough to tend to the president's wounds when he got into a fight with his wife.

He forgot all his duties toward the nation—like promoting prosperity for all citizens. Instead, he had become the subject of his queen lover.

He bent to all her requests. It even seemed like, if he could, he would offer her the presidency. That's how good she was at satisfying every carnal needs of the so-called head of state.

The table was turned. She became the commander, and the president was subject to her laws. That woman had the power to destroy any man—might they be president, king, or emperor.

Just by looking at her, he would experience ecstasy, and when he kissed her, his whole body would feel the highest form of joy and jubilation.

That is, in few words, the chaotic situation of a slowly drifting country, and all because its president fell heads over heels in love.

Frankly, he was excessive in his decisions, and his balance was broken. The president ignored the old saying that "perfect reason escapes all extremes and calls for wisdom in sobriety."

It's a big mistake in his part, and it was going to be fatal to him. It was undoubtedly the end of his reign.

Shouldn't he show moderation in order not to regret some of his excesses while conquering the world?

It was hard to understand how such a blessed man could so easily surrender to his passions when it would have been so much better for him to exercise some self-control.

In order to reach the nirvana and taste its sweet nectar, he needed to step out of the erotic barriers of love. He preferred to lose himself in the excesses of lust. He would have been better left to an evil fate.

In his case, we could wonder whether he had free will.

He could have changed his mind anytime and avoided falling when he was at the top as president. So much success to let go of—all because he wasn't able to control his passions.

Before talking about it and severely judging him, we needed to hear his arguments, if only he had any, for at one point, he fell into his passions without remission. He was lost out of his mind.

Maybe he would acknowledge his mistakes when he is confronted with them.

Indeed he ignored his enemies who had proofs that could cost him the presidency. He was completely oblivious and kept having carefree fun with his mistress who hadn't told him she revealed all his secrets with supporting evidence.

The accused could not deny that it was his voice that was heard during the recorded effusions.

What makes a woman strong is her weakness, and what makes a man weak is his supposed strength. Still, men keep considering themselves as the stronger sex and women as the weaker sex. This is completely false because in addition to the sweet words she had pictures to go with the sound, the president will have no chance when it comes to his enemies from the opposition.

Women are the queen of intimate relations, and men are their valets, might they be presidents or emperors.

The great French poet Corneille put it best when he said: "Despite the greatness of the kings, they are just like us."

It doesn't matter if a man is president or a simple citizen. When a man is in love, he is neither able to measure his weakness nor the capacities of his woman.

Some men crawl when their wives threaten to cut off intimacy. Any president becomes an ordinary man who longs for carnal pleasures. He can be reduced to his simplest expression, that is to say, a degree below zero while his partner takes pride in her capacity to remain dignified.

Our man was on the brink of losing everything, walking so close to the edge of the cliff. He had entered a maze and was unable to find the breadcrumbs that would lead him to the exit.

CHAPTER 7

The Beginning of the Impeachment Process

This was a golden opportunity to overthrow the leader who was unmatched since the existence of the USA.

A leader of that caliber would have surely been reelected as many times as the Constitution allowed to the point that there was no need of an opposition. They could never nominate a candidate that would be able to beat him.

If they ever did, it would only be to amuse the gallery. The opposition candidate would only be a laughingstock of the American people.

Indeed, next to such a popular leader, he would have no chance of winning. It was unthinkable; even in his dreams, he could not win.

Consequently, the opposition harbored a lot of hostility towards the president. They looked for a way to prevent him from being reelected.

It was impossible to compete with the people's favorite. It was like the presidency was his by right. Even his handpicked successors would benefit from his popularity.

His legacy would last forever.

This is not make-believe. It is reality. You don't need to be a genius to easily see this. Impeaching him would be near impossible since the president was still very popular.

Therefore, one can understand the importance of these tapes. They are going to be used to easily prove the president's sexual immorality.

In stating these facts with concrete evidence to support them, no lawyer or group of lawyers could get him out of trouble.

He was stuck and had no way to get out of it, especially since a president should be a role model, not a womanizer and an insatiable man, thirsting over women.

His abuses appeared to be a shame for the world-leading economic, military, and scientific power. Outside of the country, some American citizens are even embarrassed to identify as such. because they are being quizzed about their leader's scandalous behavior.

However, when it was time to show a passport, one could nolonger hide his or her nationality.

As for the president, he preferred to live a quiet life instead of being ashamed or even sent to jail.

In this context, the opposition was very happy to have a way to oust the president before the end of his term. They had to take advantage of the situation.

They needed to immediately seize the ball and use the scandal against their rival to force him to abdicate—since a pervert has no place at the White House.

They thought that such a crime would encourage the people to get to the streets and chase him out of the White House. It was a staggering blow carried in the heart of the country and the world. They needed to act fast.

After consultation, the senior members of the opposition party agreed that these tapes proving the immorality of the president were more than enough to impeach him.

The media—including radio, print, and television—relayed the news. So did the Internet and social networks.

Some posters were plastered all over the country to denigrate this rascal who was once so popular. The shame was both national and international.

Some investigative journalists seized this sensational news. They made contact by phone or via intermediaries to some White House employees. They were offered substantial financial compensation for their testimony, but none of them accepted. They proved to be extremely discreet, keeping to themselves this open secret.

News organizations faced, nonetheless, a major challenge. The witnesses were scarce and scared to substantiate their claims. Many people had doubts concerning the truthfulness of these allegations. That's why these largely broadcasted news started being considered as defamatory.

Many remained attached to their president despite his sexual mishaps. How lucky he was!

Even in deep trouble, he was protected by some supernatural force. Once again, he was favored like no other by tutelary gods.

The press then risked being sued and having to pay huge sums of money to the chief of state who, in reality, was consumed by guilt and completely lost in sexual immorality.

In the streets, the reactions were immediate. The press had misled the people. They dared to try and discredit the president, in vain. They could not tarnish the honor of such popular man. They were even being accused of serving the opposition party to oust him. They were in deep trouble and seen their credibility questioned.

Once again, the president came out unstained from sharp criticisms. Words fail to express the fierce vehemence of the press organs, which nonetheless had authentic tapes.

They were even accused of faking or imitating the president's voice to degrade and humiliate him, for the words of his staff were relevant. They claimed the president, who was a righteous and genuine man, has never ever had extramarital affairs.

He managed to come out of all this commotion even more popular in the eye of the people. He took this as an opportunity to improve his image which, in reality, was never tarnished.

In a speech on TV, he presented himself as a poor victim of a baseless plot to get rid of him.

Live from the White House's Oval Office and while the whole nation clung on to their screens and all TV channels, all media from all over the world were broadcasting his appearance. The president said the following words:

My fellow citizens and people all around the world, I greet you warmly with equanimity.

I've been so loved by my people who propelled me to power with an unprecedented majority in the history of our republic. So I can understand the relentless attacks on my honor by my critics. They are inventing fabricated allegations about extramarital affairs.

They have very fertile imaginations, for they don't have other ways of reducing my popularity to my people. My brightness and confidence would never be tarnished by those who have been bribed.

My critics are fishermen in trouble waters.

Why don't they join me in elevating this country and reach an ideal? We need to reach for the sky if we want to live in the vicinity of God.

They are just hungry for power. Why don't they wait the next election to compete with me? Because they know, given the strong attachment of the voters for their leader, they have no chance of becoming president.

My plan for a second term is already set in motion.

During my short time in the White House, real changes already take place, thanks to a dynamic team that sticks to my policies focusing on education, morality, technology, systematic development.

The progress is tangible. Not to brag, since I consider myself as a mere servant who barely started his mission for the people. I plan on not only being a role model to my people but to everyone else in the world.

As a beneficiary of the light, I'm going to use it to enlighten the darkness to such extent that at the end of my first term, in comparison with my predecessors, people will see the evolution in all aspects of their lives.

With care, skill, and dedication, I'm fighting tooth and nails to find the best methods ever used to propel the United States of America in places beyond imagination and satisfy everyone needs beyond their hopes and aspirations.

I insist that education should be free at all levels. That way, young people are to be encouraged not to drop out of school because the quality of a nation is measured through its youth. They will have to be in charge, sooner or later.

The young people who have gone astray due to drugs will be enrolled in rehab programs to help them with their sobriety and studies. This way, when they get out, they will find jobs to avoid recidivism risks.

Education must be privileged, for it's the key to dignity. Morality should be a part of the program as early as kindergarten to prevent children from being corrupted. Immorality should be corrected.

Let's all work together to put forward these citizen actions for the common good!

Let's be united, not to denigrate each other, but to help.

Let everyone bring a brick for the construction of this shining city on the hill that is America.

I have many more projects for the country, but we need a serene and quiet environment. We need social and political stability.

Peace is a prerequisite to development and progress. That's why I'm calling for the patriotic forces of the country.

I ask them to forget about their personal ambitions and think about the more important interests of the nation.

The government will take strong measures against those who threaten public peace.

I have faith in this newfound unity, not to destroy honest people's reputation, for it's easy to destroy and so difficult to build.

Let us choose to built our nation around unity and strengthen our position in the world. The only way forward is to unite all the sons and daughters of our common nation.

God bless you, and God bless the United States of America.

Chapter 8

Other Proceedings by the Opposition to Impeach the President

With his threatening speech, the president thought he would scare the people and especially his political adversaries. But his speech only had the opposite effect—it galvanized the opposition.

Media commentators and political analysts castigated the president who was seen as having dictatorial inclinations.

His weakness made him even more vulnerable. More than a dozen women appeared on the press with stories about the president. A file was made by Congress which was dominated by the opposition party.

All radio stations and TV channels allocated most of their airtime to the outrageous behavior of the chief of state. This climate of tension led to many conversations within the population.

Nevertheless, there was still hope. His supporters wished to find a new recourse to at least allow him to keep his functions.

He thought that the prosecutions would ultimately lead to something, but in reality, the opposition party was not ready to consider itself defeated.

He would come back to attack because as the old saying goes, "There is no smoke without fire."

The opposition party was determined to defeat the man that no candidate wanted to compete with during the elections. Therefore, the only solution was to request the attorney general to hire an independent prosecutor to investigate the shameful scandals around the head of state. Attempting to impeach such a popular head of state was a major challenge.

Faced with so much insistence, a zealous and independent prosecutor was hired to deal with the thorny issue with unlimited budget.

A gang of great detectives was also hired to assist him in his complicated task. They put together a list of former employees who were fired.

Some of them managed to find new jobs, others were still unemployed. They were approach with courtesy and kindly asked to testify under oath.

During the investigation, there were convincing testimonies about the first mistress of the president, and we learned about the frequency of their meetings in the Oval Office, especially when the First Lady was not around. Many said the same thing.

One of the investigators managed to obtain prime intelligence, namely, the identity of one of the bodyguards of the man who was so adored then.

Though he was fired, he was still discreetly receiving a salary in exchange for his silence in case the president is in trouble. He was contacted in his birth state, and two investigators went there to question him.

He revealed everything he saw and heard and confessed that he enjoyed tremendous benefits: for both closely guarding the president and keeping his mouth shut. He confessed he was uncomfortable when working at the White House. As a security professional, he did not understand why his job was reduced to monitoring and covering acts of adultery by the commander in chief.

He was thanked for his firsthand information. They offered him compensation, but he refused.

"Do you know any other former employees that could help us?"

"Of course."

He gave them the names of two other former employees.

The investigation was moving steadily. The two other men were contacted, and one of them was asked, "Do you have any information about intimate relations regarding the president and the intern?"

"Who are you talking about?"

"The president's mistress."

"He had one? Well, not to my knowledge."

"Why were you fired without compensation? Can you give me the reason for that?"

"I think the president simply found it better to fire me. It was his choice. I don't have to wonder about his reasons. Especially since I have assets, like my diploma, to help me find a job with a bigger salary than the one I had at the White House." I would say he rendered me a service.

"Did you find one?"

"I sent my resume all over the world."

"What are the results?"

"I'm embarrassed with choices."

"I've got at least ten interviews on the phone, and employers are willing to pay me double the salary I had at the White House."

"In what domain?"

"I have a master's degree in computer science."

"I understand the enthusiasm of employers."

"This past year, I've been preparing for my doctorate online. In less than a year, I'm sure I will pass the final exam with honors and obtain my doctorate."

"Thanks for having us."

"I'm at your disposal, but don't count on me regarding the intimate relations of a man, might they be king or emperor. They are humans like us, and humans are weak, especially in that area."

The investigator and his team moved to the second former White House employee.

He would maybe give them certain elements to put a compromising file together in order to trap the president and force him to resign.

That was the objective of the opposition party.

The day of the meeting, the names of the respondents were sealed. It was probably not to compromise them because the president was still in power, therefore, still influential. His authority has not diminished.

"I'm here on behalf of the independent prosecutor, and we are investigating the intimate relations between the president and an intern."

"I know her."

"But what do you know about her relations to the commander in chief?"

"She was very, very close to him, if you catch my drift."

"Was she often with the president?"

"At least three times a day during office hours. Once inside, you could sometimes hear the two lovers laughing and moaning."

"It's general disorder."

"More like presidential disorder."

"Are you willing to testify, in case of trial?"

"Why would I be afraid to tell the truth?"

"Aren't you afraid of retaliation?"

"Not at all. With the relevance of my testimonies, there is no doubt he would be caught. In addition to being impeached, if the First Lady sues him for adultery, he risks spending some years in prison."

"Do you wish that?"

"Certainly. Because a president should be a model of righteousness, not a vile womanizer. If he cannot control himself, how could he then manage his administration? When the nation is sure of his adultery with concrete evidence, people will express their regret for having elected such scum."

"Are you ready to collaborate with us and help inform people about the president's forfeit? Given the state of the investigation, we have accumulated so much evidence! To the point that we could annihilate him for his crimes. However, the head of state is a very skillful man. He has infiltrated, through third parties, the different phases of the investigation, to such extent that we are at the edge of an abyss. He will also use the power at his discretion to prevent his impeachment, especially since his former lover is willing to collaborate."

The thought of that news made him shiver.

The First Lady, seeing the hell in which her husband was in, decided to intervene. If he thought that his illicit dating would make such a fuss, he would have abstained from it, that's for sure.

Let's also give him mitigating circumstances. He started suffering from chronic insomnia. During his sleepless nights, the First Lady, in her generosity, would try to console him so that he could regain his composure. How kind of her.

Maybe she was only motivated by her need to remain First Lady. It was a title of high rank that she wished to keep. Therefore, why not stand on her husband's side and help him get through this storm in the White House. In her mind, that was the right move.

She was even ready to defend him tooth and nails against all his so-called adversaries, opponents, or enemies. She then started perfectly controlling her jealousy to make sure he's not caught. She agreed to be a team player.

Indeed she benefited from covering him. Any of her contributions would help her husband to get out of this mess. That's why she was ready to declare that they never slept in separate bedrooms and that her husband has always been faithful.

Such a declaration would not be enough to convince people compared to the compelling evidences the investigators had.

Indeed, the opposition party vowed to get him out by all means necessary. Such circumstances were more derogatory than embarrassing.

One night, while her husband was suffering from insomnia, the First Lady jumped to remind him who he was.

"Aren't you the president of the United States of America? Aren't you the most powerful man in the world? I always wanted to marry a man who has balls, your attitude is pathetic. No one will help you. No one will prevent your government from falling into disgrace. Your enemies are plotting in broad daylight, and you're the only one that doesn't see it. You are being unbelievably passive right now. If you don't act quickly, very soon, you'll be old news. You must neutralize these power-hungry people. Only you can save yourself and the presidency. The large majority of the people who got you in power are waiting for you to do something and do it quick. The people are with you. Did you forget that the voice of the people is also the voice of God?"

His head full with his wife's harangue. The president took a path of no return. Conscious of the extent of his powers, he had to toughen his position in order to save his government and remain in power. He was ready for action.

· In the morning he summoned an extraordinary meeting at the White House, in the Situation Room or the "bunker," with his vice president, his national security adviser, his secretaries of justice, defense, the secretary of state, the members of the joint chiefs of staff, the FBI and CIA directors, the Marshals Service director, and everyone else that he needed to set up his Machiavellian plan.

CHAPTER 9

The Noose is Tightening Around the President as He Toughens His Position

Knowing that the intern was ready to collaborate and reveal her affair with the president, he felt like the end was near, especially since it was possible that the girlfriend had some compromising photos.

At this stage, he was tormented. He struggled and did anything in his power to get out of this maze. He even made arrangements to introduce some drastic measures. In doing so, he didn't know he was making things worse.

Was he tortured by remorse? No one could tell, for no one would dare ask him. People would know if in his memoirs he decided to write about his love crimes.

In reality, he had no interest in talking about it. He would have risked a posthumous sentence from a judgment in absentia, which is the act of judging a dead person for crimes they perpetrated when alive.

There was a time when he tried to put all odds on his side to clear himself. That was a dream that have never happened. Despite his unpleasant situation, he was going to gamble it all because you never know what the future holds. Some miracle can happen and save him from destitution.

There might be a way out; at least it was a possibility, even though it was farfetched. If he had a good relationship with God, he would have asked him to turn the impossible to possible.

According to this hypothesis, we could assume that God, the embodiment of justice, would not get himself involved in this lustful situation. Therefore, he could not count on the Eternal to hide his disgusting crime of adultery. He needs advices or to simply hear the opinions of his closest collaborators. Everyone gave him advices to the best of their abilities.

"Your Excellency, in my humble opinion, we should infiltrate the investigators hired on the case. They might, to some extent, be useful to us. They could reveal to us what they know." said the national security adviser.

"How will I do that?"

"By feeding them information regarding alleged things about you."

"What if they use that to better trap me?"

"It's one possible hypothesis."

"Given my status, I must be extremely careful to avoid losing ground to my opponents."

"You're right. In that case, my proposal is dangerous. It could compromise you even more."

"What about you, vice president, what do you think? What do you advice me to do?"

"It's going to be hard to escape this unscathed. We must hire a consortium of well-known lawyers, specialists in cases of senior officials' misconducts. I promise you I will undertake some research in that direction, and in three days, at the latest, I will try and communicate to you a list of specialist lawyers in this field, because this is a truly important case."

"What do you mean by that?"

"Your Excellency, you are the head of state. People accuse you of adultery, and the news has already been all around the world. All the major foreign newspapers made it their front page news, especially in France, England, and Germany."

"Can I see those newspapers?"

"I advise you not to look at them. They'll just get you upset. Both your picture and the intern's are displayed everywhere. It would be better not to think about it and let the lawyers advice you on the best way to get out of trouble.

We also need to act fast, since we don't know when they will start the impeachment process."

The president became red after hearing those words, like he received a cold shower. He remained silent for a moment. After he got himself together, he asked his secretary of justice's opinion.

"Personally, I agree with the vice president, and frankly, I don't know how you could get out of this scandal. Let's call it as it is. In such circumstances, to be completely honest, it will be impossible to maintain you in power."

"How dare you speak like that?"

"I'm just being honest, not beating round the bush. I speak from heart. Time to be honest. You are accused of adultery. More than a crime, it's a forfeit, especially since it's committed by a sitting president. Therefore, one can wonder if there is a solution to that. This is a serious crime, and according to people, you are still very fond of women's treasures. Some employees are saying that you undress them with your eyes."

"Thank you for honest words. Now, it's time for me to make a decision, and contrary to what you all think, I have the solution. As the commander of the public force, I plan on using it in such circumstances. I am the supreme leader, and I plan on staying until the end of my term, and no one can stop me."

"But, Your Excellency, we are in a democracy, any undemocratic move on your will make my job very difficult, not to say impossible" replied the white house lawyer .

"Since when the people exercised power? said the President, Democracy is an empty word. Moreover, the Greek author, Demosthenes, the greatest political scientist of all time, rightly called the people *the many*, or the *the rabble*. Contrary to popular belief, this term is not Voltaire's, it's a translation of *the many*. Therefore, since the people are ignorant, the person who was chosen to lead them should act with only the superior interests of the nation in mind.

"The nation is under threat. I have to do something to rid it of all scum and make sure that every citizen is safe before a handful of scumbags disturb the peace. My mind is made and the country in the right hands. . . mine. Don't worry, your president is capable of rising up to the task.

"I'm not scared. I'm going to take some drastic measures, and very soon, the plotters and their schemes will be old news.

"The unity of the nation must be protected against all odds. We need to set the record straight and start working together again. We must be completely committed to fighting people who want to destroy us.

"I shall rise up to the task. You can count on my undying devotion for the welfare of this country. Our situation is not yet hopeless. Don't be afraid. Your captain will lead the boat to safety, despite the storm. Just be calm. Great sailors rise up to the task when the sea is rough with strong and destructive winds."

Those who were gathered started getting confident again due to the comforting words of the commander in chief. Deep inside, everyone was wondering how he was going to go about calming down such a scandal.

The president stood up and said:

"Exceptional situations call for exceptional measures. We need to protect our democratic traditions. It's our duty not to surrender to blackmail, to false allegations by people who are hungry for power and know that they can't get it through elections against a president as popular as I am. They may say and do whatever they want. Their plans are bound to fail.

"The power will remain in the hands of the one that it was given to. In other words, I was elected for four years, and the Constitution allows me to run for a second term.

"I can already see myself being reelected, thanks to my popularity. Nothing, nobody can harm my government. They can't make me step down. With the people behind me and my popularity at it's peak, they won't dare going through with their so called impeachment. They are dreaming if they think so.

"I believe in my destiny. I will elevate this country to a nation of real patriots united in love. Whoever dares to go against the will of the people will fail miserably"..."

"But Your Excellency, what are you planning to do?" asked the chairman of the joint chief of staff.

"Let's wait and see. I have the solution and, very soon, all these plots against me will be completely annihilated. They will become old news.

"As the commander in chief, I intend to use my discretionary power to put those who try to derail my presidency in line. They will be neutralized.

"First, I will take drastic measures to restore serenity in people's minds.

"Some people, not to say a lot, will be punished with the utmost rigor, because you cannot make an omelet without breaking eggs.

"There will be zero tolerance. A series of measures will be taken, and get ready to answer the many questions the media will ask you.

"We must all stick together. Your solidarity with the government is required.

"In the next twenty four hours, I will address the nation to announce the exceptional measures that we have to take to save our national integrity and democratic traditions for which our ancestors fought and died for.

"This will be the most important address in our entire nation's history."

"You dare to go that far?" asked the director of the FBI.

"It's just a matter of hours. I've made my mind, and as the president of the leading economic, military, and scientific country that humanity has ever known, we must understand that desperate times call for desperate measures, even if they go against public opinion."

"Such measures are antidemocratic. Everyone should act according to the law. It doesn't matter who you are. This is anticonstitutional. This will be considered high treason. It's an impeachable crime," said the Attorney General.

"To succeed in doing this, the right procedure is to use Congress. Only Congress can constitute itself into the high court of justice to judge a sitting President. However, that will not be possible since, very soon, there won't be a Congress."

"Your Excellency, you're exceeding your rights now." Said the secretary of state.

"That's not true, because when the higher interests of the nation are threatened, we must do all we can to remedy the problem. Know that all constitutions are drafted by the constituents and, over time, if faced with changing circumstances these laws no longer reflect reality, then we have to change them to include more suited amendments.

"As the commander in chief, I'll take my responsibilities. I don't care what people say, and I am going to control the situation that might lead to anarchy. Therefore, prevention is better than cure. We must act before it's too late. The history books will remember me as a president who had the courage to take the necessary measures to protect the higher interests of the American people.

"As the last bastion of democracy, I am aware of my responsibility to lead our country to a higher destiny. It is undeniable that the only way to access the presidency is and always will be through elections by universal suffrage.

"As for me, I was elected president with a strong majority. Therefore, the people gave me a sacred mandate to defend their interests at all costs. We are past talking about things. Now is the time to act because the situation is getting worse by the minute.

"Each of you gathered here will have a role to play to preserve our government and institutions.

"To you, Mr. Secretary of Justice, you shall issue an arrest warrant against the independent prosecutor who caused all this mess. He is the number one enemy of the nation. There won't be a solution to this crisis as long as this man is free.

"The director of the FBI will make sure the warrant is executed in the next twenty-four hours before my address to the nation.

"Mr. US Marshals Director, your service is necessary because public buildings like the Capitol and the Supreme Court will go under the control of your agents right before my message to the nation tomorrow evening at eight p.m. They will keep them closed until further notice.

"As for you members of the joint chief of staff, the army, the navy, as well as the air force, must be in code D and be ready to intervene immediately if necessary to restore order.

"I ask for a dozen armored tanks to be stationed around the White House perimeter immediately and, to avoid outbursts, I ask that by six p.m. tomorrow, four marine battalions start patrolling the streets of Washington to reinforce the local police.

"As for you, Mr. Secretary of State, I need you to contact all our embassies and the foreign ministries of our main allies to inform them about the situation. Contact the United Nations secretary-general, the secretary-general of the OAS, the prime mister of Canada, the Vatican, the prime minister of Great Britain, the French president, and the German chancellor to reassure them and explain to them that the decisions that would be implemented in the next twenty-four hours are temporary. America will undoubtedly remain the leader of the free world."

Few discordant voices were heard, but the president paid them no mind. He made them understand that his decision was made and that no deviation would be tolerated within the government.

At 11:00 p.m., the meeting ended, and the participants left with heavy hearts and demoralized, but they decided to follow the orders of the president.

The next day, a tense atmosphere prevailed in the country. All TV channels, radio broadcasts, social networks, and press agencies were talking about the explosive situation of the country.

Meanwhile, the Congress deliberated and obtained the required majority to initiate the process of impeachment of the president.

It was 1:00 p.m. when the White House spokesman in a press conference announced to journalists and the American people that the president had an important message for the nation. He will deliver it this evening at 8:00 p.m.

People started speculating immediately. Some thought the president was going to resign to avoid humiliation and impeachment, but this would be to underestimate that man. He had a taste of power and could not see himself outside this position that gave him access to unimaginable honors and privileges.

CHAPTER 10

Important Message to the Nation

It was 7:30 p.m., eastern standard time, and all media in America, as well as most in the rest of the world, interrupted their regular programs to give the air to commentators and American politic experts. They were all speculating about the future of the United States if the president steps down or is impeached.

For the majority of these experts, there was no third possibility. They could not have imagined what they were about to hear in the following minutes.

It was 7:55 p.m. when a signal from the White House showed the podium with the big presidential seal, "President of the United States," the microphone, and of course, the teleprompter.

It was 8:00 p.m., Eastern Standard Time, when the president made his appearance. With a serene face, he began his speech as usual with the following words:

My fellow Americans, tonight I think it's time to address you directly because my presidency is the fruit of your trust in me and in my ability to govern.

Our great nation is going through hard times because the forces of darkness are plotting to destroy our democratic, social, and political traditions.

For some time now, an atmosphere of division and instability lurks in our country.

Some traditional politicians prefer to mortgage the future of our country to benefit their own petty interests. They do not hesitate to undermine our democratic foundations only to satisfy their ambitions and accomplish what they could not do through elections.

Therefore, these lost souls think they could disturb the public peace with unfounded rumors to smear the image of your president. They want to mess the people's mind up and bring chaos to the country.

They will fail because the defender of the people's democratic power will stand strong as a rampart to their treacheries.

Congress, which used to be the mecca of great legislative and democratic debate, is today only a shadow of what it was.

Today, it is the den of envious and power-hungry politicians ready to sacrifice the higher interests of the nation for their personal ambitions. They are empty tanks.

Their Machiavellian plan will fail miserably. Their project, which is awfully treacherous and vain, is already doomed. I'm asking you, my fellow Americans, to remain calm and be vigilant.

To stop this descent to hell that threatens our great country, to prevent the disintegration of our institutions and keep our democratic tradition, I find myself in the painful obligation to take the following decrees. . .

Article one, the Constitution is suspended until further notice.

Article two, the United States Congress is immediately dissolved, and new elections to elect a new body of competent and patriotic legislators will be held as soon as possible. Article three, the five members of the Supreme Court over seventy years old are thanked for their service to the nation and are retired.

Article four, the news media in all its forms will practice self-censorship and will avoid sensationalism by spreading rumors and false information that may disturb public order.

Article five, as of tonight, the National Guard in all fifty states will fall under the control of the federal government.

Article six, martial law is declared throughout the district of Washington and its suburbs.

Security forces will reprimand with rigor any offender.

I hope these measures will only be temporary and, at the right time, after evaluating the situation, I promise to gradually repeal them.

God bless the United States of America. God bless the brave American people.

CHAPTER 11

Reactions of Rage and Outcry

By acting this way, the culprit hoped to exculpate himself. Instead, he caused a scandal more destructive than his adulterous act.

If he was a responsible leader, he would submit to the rigorous condemnation of the law. He went beyond his rights and made things worse.

Did he hope to calm the tensions and control this explosive situation with his tyrannical and anti-democratic measures? Instead, he caused an unprecedented social and political explosion.

People reacted in a never-seen way in the history of a nation.

In the United States, all media, without exception, protested with outrage against this joke of a president.

They swore not to obey the person some are now calling a space alien.

Others were calling him crazy and maniac. People called for civil disobedience. Editorials asked the president to repeal these tyrannical measures and to resign immediately.

Radio and TV stations were overwhelmed with phone calls from an enraged population. They were calling for the formation of militias in every town and suburb of the country to fight this tyrant.

The next day, the headlines were: "Presidential coup,""A tyrant at the White House,""A space alien among us,""Insanity at the White House," etcetera.

Reaction at the UN

The Security Council of the United Nations met exceptionally to analyze the situation in the United States. They issued a statement condemning without reservation any act that undermines democracy, regardless of the country.

The UN reminded the US government of its role as the leader of the world and mentioned its fear that this bad example is followed by other countries with less democratic traditions.

The world organization asked for the respect of institutions, the restoration of the Constitution, and the cancellation of all anti-democratic measures taken by the US government.

The secretary-general offered his help to the American people for a quick resolution of this crisis.

The ambassador of an eastern European superpower who was in the past targeted by the US government for his totalitarian practices demanded the UN headquarters to be moved from the United States because they were no longer worthy to house such a prestigious organization like the United Nations.

Representatives of some countries where democracy was a completely unknown concept took advantage of the situation to vilify the United States, calling it hypocritical for its former positions regarding human rights and democracy.

The representatives of the US delegation simply left the chamber since their justifications for the behavior of their government in Washington didn't convince anyone. They could no longer stand all the charges and accusations against their government.

Reaction of the Organization of American States (OAS)

The Organization of American States' headquarter is located in Washington. Therefore, it was in an extremely delicate situation.

All its members were summoned to discuss the American crisis. They vigorously condemned this interruption of the great democratic tradition of the United State.

The organization reminded its member states their obligation to abide by the principles of the organization's charter, namely, the strict compliance with democratic standards and the inviolability of the parliamentary and judicial institutions.

A representative member from Latin America who had some issues with Washington asked the General Assembly to simply expel the United States from the organization.

The secretary-general of the organization said, "Given the extremely serious situation the United States is facing right now, I want this assembly to sit In permanence until the crisis is resolved in Washington."

All the countries in the Americas then recalled their ambassadors in Washington for consultation. All the chancelleries wrote press releases expressing their concerns regarding the breach of democracy by the American government.

Reactions from the Rest of the World

The European Union, the African Union, the Arab League, and the Organization of Southeast Asian Countries were unanimous in condemning the interruption of democracy in America. They demanded that constitutional order be restored immediately in America.

They invited the American government to reconsider and resume its role as the leader of the world.

Newspapers from all over the world condemned the measures taken by the American executive. Their editorials didn't hesitate to blame the American president who they compared to one of the worst tyrants in history.

Their caricatures did not hesitate to mock the American president. One of them drew him naked in the middle of a crowd of women giving him advice.

They had fertile imaginations and handled the brush with angelic dexterity.

These degrading images circulated in social media. The news was spreading fast. In this regard, the editor of a French daily wrote: "If the American president is not stopped in his follies, the country is on the verge of becoming a pariah state. What is the Army waiting for to take action? It's time for the Army to intervene and bring back democracy."

The comments on social media were even more aggressive towards the president. He was called names that I'm not going to mention here for fear of offending the sensibility of the reader.

The sitting US president was called an adulterer and a dictator.

He was ridiculed all over the world.

Reactions in the United States

All trade union organizations in the United States signed a vehement press release denouncing these dictatorial and unimaginable decisions in their country.

They issued an ultimatum to the president—either within forty-eight hours he gets himself back on track by receding all his stupid decrees, or they will paralyze the country with an indefinite generalized strike.

The New York stock market lost two thousand points in twenty-four hours. The dollar lost one-third of its value. Investors were panicking to the idea of their portfolio being completely wiped out. Students in universities and high schools threatened to close the schools if these measures were not immediately repealed. Churches of all confessions, synagogues, social and charitable organizations—all condemned unreservedly the hijacking of the democratic apparatus by the American president.

The population, from large cities to small villages, took to the streets and blocked the traffic to ask for the president's resignation. Business activities were slowing down to a level that was never seen.

The security forces were powerless, and most of them refused to intervene. Chaos spread nationwide, and a sense of feeling of rage and irritation was born in the hearts of the American people.

Some veterans even spoke openly of their desire to storm the White House and kick out that tyrant in the making.

CHAPTER 12

Inside the White House

The president had no intention of abandoning or reversing his anti-democratic and dictatorial measures. He was behaving already like a monarch by dissolving the parliament. That way, there was no way of controlling the head of the executive, that is to say, the president. Even in democracy, the president had discretionary powers.

Even though power must stop power, the fact remains that presidents have much more power than the other branches of government. But dissolving Congress and sending home Supreme Court justices, this one was just stepping way out of the norms.

Also, to make sure he remains commander in chief, he simply became a supreme leader. He not only showed very clearly his intention to lead the country alone, but he revealed the extent of his powers.

He took things further, becoming as a result a super, powerful man that rejected point-blank any form of democracy, even in its embryonic stage. He didn't even show guilt after he sinned. He had no remorse.

After having committed a shameful crime in the eyes of the nation, he took drastic steps to cover it. However, there were limits never to be crossed.

While the country was in turmoil, the atmosphere inside the White House was more than tense. The president stood completely frozen in front of the TV and computer screens to follow the reactions of the people in the country and around the world.

He ordered all White House staff to do the same and report to him every fifteen minutes. In this context, it was impossible to concentrate on anything else. He completely forgot about his love for women let alone his duties as head of state.

He became, unknowingly and unintentionally, a disillusioned man. He was in pain, emotionally and physically. He lost his manhood of yesteryear. It didn't matter what caliber of woman was in front of him.

Without a doubt, he was tortured in his palace. He was cooking in his own sauce. He was wondering about the commitment of the armed forces—if they will keep following their commander in chief. He feared a military coup, he feared for his life.

Such hypothesis was not inconsiderable, even in this democratic country (which was no longer so), since the president not only saw himself as an absolute monarch, he was also a dictator and a tyrant.

He opened the door to all sorts of anti-democratic behavior. He quickly realized his inability to execute and enforce his unconstitutional and illegal decrees.

He started to be quite frustrated. He had to battle in a melee with no enemy—to his own demise. He has been sowing wind, but when the storm came, he was scared and bordered on panicking.

When things got worse, who should he count on? Who would support him?

Previously, he was supported by the entire population. After his slippages, both sexual and political, his situation became unstable and his supporters getting fewer.

In his disarray, he questioned his survival because his conscience was telling him he was wrong. He wanted to be able to just ignore it, but he was forced to listen.

Everyone left him. He was cooking in his own sauce. He regretted his carnal sins and remembered his errors that led to the death of his soul. He would have liked to clear the table, unfortunately, his actions left an indelible impression.

The decrees were also written in stone, the writing was on the wall. He wished he was able to turn back time, but what could he do, in reality?

That was the hard question he was asking himself. There was no way of forgetting what happened. His thoughts were so troubled that he could not sleep to restore his physical and mental forces.

Day and night, his mind was tormented by his crimes. Even if a tribunal came to clear him, deep inside, he knew he will always feel guilty. To him, his crimes were unforgivable.

Since he considered himself as an alien, a thousand times greater than any man, he thought that even in the chaos of power he could turn things around.

Maybe he thought he was special, like a lost angel on earth.

At the slightest scandal, he would have won the heavens and joined God. Following a calculation that lacked basic common sense, he got lost in broad daylight. He was invaded by darkness even in the middle of the day, when the sun was at its zenith.

Therefore, when came the night, he would remain still—deprived of the slightest glimmer that would allow him to move.

There was darkness around, beyond, and especially inside him. What could he do to get out of this mess?

He was small, tiny, and infinitesimal. He was about to be reduced to his simplest form. He was regarded as the man that soon would only be the shadow of the person he used to be. He dissolved trying to be strong. He was then reduced to his simplest form, to such extent that he was unable to sleep or eat. His diet consisted of cigars and vodka.

At night, when he was in bed next to the First Lady, his wife who has not abandoned him, he would turn his back at her because he had become impotent.

Was it the beginning of his punishment by nature? No human being can answer such thorny question. The First Lady would attempt to revive him, in vain. She wanted to console him one way or another.

He was already dreading at what was going to happen to him. In my humble opinion, he was destabilized. How could he not be? Unless he completely lost his mind. He was still able think rationally.

What should I do? he wondered.

He considered all the possible outcomes. No doubt he was going to be torn apart maybe not physically but morally.

Knowing that he had no reason to live, if he wasn't watched by his wife and bodyguards, he would have tried to kill himself. That would have been the third unthinkable scandal, but he was not desperate enough to do such degrading act.

A suicide due to adultery and dictatorial measures in the United States! They may not be valid reasons, but they are enough to hate oneself and want to self-destruct.

"Savants consuls!" said the Romans.

The consuls must be careful. They must take precautions every time, day, and night. They must avoid exposing themselves to criticisms provoked by senseless, reprehensible, and unreasonable actions.

In this context, self-respect is law to avoid falling to temptation.

Once you commit a reprehensible act, the right attitude is to get yourself together and commit to never do it again. Otherwise, we run the risk of sinking into a series of bad decisions that can have irreversible results.

The president could have, after failing the first time, gotten himself together and only commit to his wife.

The sin of the flesh, committed several times, was fatal to him. They made the commander in chief want to undermine the democratic foundation of the USA.

You don't need to be a psychologist to guess that deep inside he regretted acting outside the norms, but it was too late. The world was too old.

For someone who managed to reach the highest stage of the republic, this was a humiliation. He simply let himself be drifted, first by love of the flesh, then by the passion for power.

He might not know the saying: "Perfect reason flees all extremities and want us to be wise and sober." He didn't need to lament after he committed such crimes. The president was in a very bad situation.

Being unable to forgive oneself is the worst punishment one can face, but for this privileged man who managed to become president of the United States of America, it was unavoidable.

It was the harsh truth, and it consumed his body, his soul, and his spirit. The president could then only count on himself. That's where the problem is.

He was disappointed he could not contain the coming wave of protest. When one sets up illegal measures, they can expect a backlash. Would he be able to resist the adverse reactions?

Only time will tell.

CHAPTER 13

The Beginning of the End

It was a real outcry.

An imminent danger threatened the most beloved form of government since it was able to provide, in mutual respect, well-being to the majority of people by prompting the rich minority to get rid of their surplus of wealth—still remaining extremely rich—and sharing it with the poor. That way, over time, they will see their misery decrease and have access to a more comfortable life.

They will then be part of the middle class and will see a reduction of the gap between the rich and those in the middle. That would also be a perfect way to lessen the class struggle between the haves and the haves not.

Reaching such a goal was only possible with the independence of the three powers of the state—equally, without one controlling the others.

Indeed, only democracy can favor the harmony necessary to get great results. That's why it's important to have mutual respect and work together to better govern the people and things. That way, every citizen will be able to feel safe physically and spiritually. This goal is more than noble— it's sacrosanct.

However, everything failed because at the top of the government, there was a dictator as president of the United States. He committed a crime satisfying his carnal appetites, and to stay in power, he thought he could just establish the worse dictatorship of his country's history.

Maybe he thought he was an absolute monarch at the head of an empire or kingdom.

In all countries and inside any borders, you will find people yearning for democracy. It is natural to work together and defend this form of government. One must fight for its survival.

The American people was going to take its responsibilities in this challenge they're facing all because of this new tyrant, named John Redlight, president of the United States of America, who seemed like a problem but was really nothing but a bad apprentice in the art of dictatorship.

He fanned the hate of his people and people all over the world upon himself. It was necessary to quickly act in concert and counter the ambitious goals of this criminal.

They had to stop him for the defense of human rights and rule of laws all over the world. Every country has the right to elect a leader whose administration is controlled by equally elected civil servants, namely deputies and senators, also known as legislators in the voting of laws in favor of their constituents. The judiciary's job is to interpret these laws.

The coordination of these three powers allows us to avoid impunity and injustice. Therefore our president, who accumulated all the powers, appeared to be drifting from the right path.

It was a national shame in the twenty-first century when countries recognize the merits of democracy with power balancing to avoid overlapping, it is inconceivable that any sane person could imagine amassing all the powers and get away with it.

The response must be quick to prevent the entire country from being poisoned. The venom needed to be neutralized, and the only antidote was the overthrowing of the president by the high court of justice that would condemn him and punish him.

The punishment needed to be exemplary so that never in this country, considered as a model of democracy, would we have such a dictator again. Such crimes should be ancient history.

He unfortunately tried to kill democracy, but the people were going to revolt because the beautiful and wonderful cannot be destroyed. You can try to destroy it, but you will fail and become completely torn. It was a vain attempt on his part. He was bound to fail ever since his Machiavellian declaration.

The ideal Sovereign is partisan of free will and doesn't impose his will on those he's supposed to save. That's why we all should model our behavior on him if we don't want damnation.

This president was a misfortune to everyone. He tried and failed to destroy the indestructible. Such enterprise was so foolish to a president who turned deaf to the calls of reason.

He wanted to take, at will or according to his fancy, a position contrary to universal norms. Standing out in stupidity turns out to be a very bad choice and based on a serious mistake.

He should have, on the contrary, reconsidered and admitted his wrongs after his first offense. Congress would have forgiven him and wouldn't have required him to be prosecuted and be removed.

In addition, his multiple offenses made him an unrepentant sinner. He became vile, falling to the point of committing a succession of political crimes—including the dissolution of the parliament, the dismissal of the Supreme Court justices, the imposition of martial law, the usurpation of people's rights and freedoms, etcetera.

CHAPTER 14

Reactions of the Congress

Exasperated by such excesses, members of the House of Representatives and the senate constituting the Congress came back to attack since their expulsion by the president was considered null and void. It was like nothing happened.

They remained during their entire term as irrevocable and irremovable officials. If while serving his duties one of them committed a crime, his colleagues would gather into a legislative tribunal, and if the allegations happened to be true, only then would they vote at a majority to remove his immunity.

Only then could he be brought to justice to answer his alleged crimes. His judgment would be in the jurisdiction where the crime was committed and in accordance with principles recognized everywhere in the world regarding these matters.

These judicial considerations prove, if proofs were necessary, that Congress remains immutable, unchangeable, and unchanged during its mandate that was assigned through elections in compliance with the Constitution.

Congress also published a properly written message to the nation, asking people to forget about the infamy done against the constitution, the nation and the Supreme Court justices and, by extension, the cancellation of the flagrant infringement on American justice.

Legally speaking, the president was unable to bribe justice by using the police to forcibly execute his unlawful wishes.

He was behaving like a supreme ruler, forgetting that according to the most fashionable political theory, in a democracy, power balances power, should we quote Montesquieu in *The Spirit of the Laws.*

There should be no overstepping.

He was ready to use blind force to destroy legalities. That way, you don't need to be a genius to understand the aforementioned principles.

Therefore, he introduced anarchy instead of good old democracy. Without a doubt, he was an anarchic president. He could not call himself a true decision maker.

Such posture belittled the president into his simplest expression. He had engaged in practices so radical that they turned him into an absolute monarch.

Absolutism is the twin sister of dictatorship in that it destroys all democratic institutions. Maybe he didn't measure the extent of his illicit and impeachable actions. He could even be imprisoned for this, not to mention face public shame.

Having put Congress and justice aside, his crimes could not remain go unpunished. He thought he was above the law. He wished to turn the White House into a palace for a dictatorial monarch.

Men, no matter their social status, their wealth or their profession are subject to the law, which is defined as "the expression of the popular will." Going against this principle is losing one's humanity. He should stay away from that and walk a loyal and righteous path in order not to feel the full force of an unforgiving law of justice.

Indeed, once you break the law, you must expect to pay the price, which can go from paying a fine to dismissal, according to your position, or even imprisonment. There was nothing more to hide. He took the mask off to appear in his nakedness as the holder of all powers.

He got rid of all constraints. Their use didn't matter, and he imposed his will *per fas et nefas*, that is to say, against all odds.

It was unbelievable to see the president of the United States of America behave so recklessly and so foolishly.

He was ignoring the great American principles, even though he knew he was bound to pay for that. He had crossed the point of no return. Never in the history of America had people thought they would see such sample of a dictator.

While their buildings were locked, sealed and guarded by deputy Marshalls, the members of Congress and the nine Supreme Court justices met in a big conference room of a great hotel in Washington DC under the lights and cameras of national and international television channels. They stayed there for a marathon session, deliberating and establishing the high court of justice that's going to judge and condemn the president dictator.

The president of the senate compared the American president to England's King George III during the revolution of the American colonies that led to their independence. He declared that day would mark their second independence from tyranny.

At the end of this urgent session, the full congress unanimously voted two articles: first, they repealed and nullified all the illegal acts of the president dictator, and then they voted to impeach both the president and the vice-president.

When, according to the Constitution, both the president and vicepresident are incapacitated or removed from office then the Speaker of the House of Representatives should ensure the interim until new elections are held. So they invited the chief justice of the Supreme Court, assisted by eight justices, to preside the swearing-in ceremony of the Speaker of the House.

TV channels that covered exclusively this unprecedented crisis announced the news live:

BREAKING NEWS!
America has a new president!

People started speculating on what would happen in the next few days. The new president, just after he took his oath, addressed the nation from the hotel where he was temporarily residing.

He started by listing the crimes committed by the former president. He then assured the nation that all institutions had stayed intact and invited everyone to resume their normal activities. He informed the international community that America is still the world's leader, and the quick resolution of this crisis is to be considered as proof of the strength and vitality of the American democratic institutions.

Here is an excerpt of his message:

My fellow Americans,

As your president in an exceptional situation, I pledge to rise to your expectations and be a president who strictly respects the laws of the republic. We are a country with democratic traditions, and nobody can violate these immutable, unchangeable, and unchanging laws.

The unfortunate events of the past days will forever leave their indelible stain on the history and the memory of our people. All the destabilizing measures taken by the former president are now null and void.

My predecessor got lost to the point that his pathetic attitude approaches that of a drug addict in the paranoia stage. He demeaned us, but the world will understand this was only a step back.

It will fade and disappear forever.

Such crimes will be buried in the minds of the current and future generations. Our institutions that were attacked will resume their normal activities as soon as tomorrow. They were rehabilitated.

The people's house, the Capitol, returned in the hands of its rightful occupants, that is to say, the senators and members of the House.

[applause from congressmen]

I just ordered the removal of the padlocks on the Supreme Court building. Now the honorable judges of that glorious Court can return immediately to the Temple of Themis. Life returns to normal, and we can rejoice that there were more fear than harm.

To the fourth power, that is the press, I want to give my special thanks for the more than noble way you did your job during these dark moments in our history. Continue your sacred mission of informing the people and defending democracy.

To the brave American people, I have never been more proud to be called American. Your fierce resistance to tyranny as well as your determination to live free or die put you in the company of heroic and immortal peoples of history. The sad episode we just experienced is a mere interlude in our glorious history.

Let's get to work to maintain our standard of living and solidify our democracy.

To the international community and to different world's organizations that rightfully were concerns regarding our country's democratic health, I want to say our democracy is stronger than ever.

I will, however, publicly present an apology on my country's behalf to anyone outside the US who was offended by these insane acts perpetuated by my predecessor. The United States will remain the undisputed leader of democracy in the world.

Finally, we want to reassure the nation that justice shall prevail. Anyone who violated the law and the Constitution of the country will face the full force of the law and be severely punished.

He finished his speech with the familiar phrase:

"God bless you and God bless the United States of America."

The New President Takes the Reins of Power

The first act of the new president was to invite members of the joint chiefs of staff at his hotel room and ordered them to bring all troops back to their barracks, strip the White House of all military protection, and reposition the armored tanks to face the White House . He ordered that the White House be cordoned off not letting anyone in our out.

The generals saluted the new president and promised to carry out his orders to the letter. The chairman contacted all division commanders and transmitted the necessary instructions regarding the retreat of the troops and their repositioning.

The White House was almost emptied of its staff since the majority of them panicked had abandoned their posts. Only the most zealous partisans of the fallen president remained loyal to him. Some had even sworn to die for him.

However, like before the storm, there was a deathly hush. Except when the media called to ask for information, the phones stopped ringing and people stopped visiting. The White House seemed lifeless.

The most outrageous rumors started floating around social media. Some were about the president fleeing to take refuge in the embassy of a communist country, while others spoke of his possible suicide.

In reality, he was still at his post awaiting his fate with the composure of a stoic.

CHAPTER 15

Reactions of the Ousted President

Seeing and hearing what just happened at the hotel, the former president felt hunted. People came to announce to him that the tanks around the White House were moving. As he looked at the window, he saw them now pointing their cannons at the White House. Panicking, he tried to escape, but there was nowhere to go.

He considered seeking refuge in a foreign country's embassy, but there was no way for him to get there and escape his country's justice. He regretted being surrounded and not being free to come and go. Deep inside, he knew it was over for him.

He was getting more and more pessimistic, he started losing his mind, and he could not find the latitude towards freedom. He was stuck, physically and morally.

His closest companions were a box of cigars that he burnt one after another and a bottle of whisky.

The malignant always manages to do deeds; that in time, will turn against him. All exits were double-locked. At this point, he was left with no possibility of salvation. He had no way of getting out of trouble.

Why did he engage in this highway to anarchy? Was he under the influence of a drug, even at a low dose?

It is difficult to understand that a leader the likes of this head of state could get so lost, he just could not be moderate in his decisions.

Was it too late to undo his crimes? It was not such a complicated question; the answer was quite obvious. He was wondering about his future. Was he not already a potential prisoner at the White House? Well, it looked like it.

He had to serve his sentence and examine his conscience. He could not stay still. He was so tormented that he was constantly moving in his room.

The First Lady was trying to comfort him somehow, but in vain. She knew that she would be deprived of the attention of her husband.

"Honey, you are disturbed in your body, your soul, and your mind. Try to rest."

"Rest? In such times, that would be lying to myself. Don't you realize the extent of my troubles? I risk life imprisonment. But I have nobody else to blame but myself. It all started with me being weak and chasing tails. How many people did I hurt in the process? I know my repentance is useless despite my sincere regrets. I know you will never forgive me, nor will I be forgiven by all those who believed in me, and I understand that perfectly."

"Don't worry."

"Oh, I would be so happy if the American people were as forgiving as you! But it is vain to hope so. Do you think I'll go to prison? I am sure they are drafting the bill of indictment right now. They will release it in the near future. *Alea acta est.* ["The die is cast."] We are lost. It's over for me. I'm dead. Quite simply, I exist with a heart devoured by the stress and remorse."

Tears started coming out of his eyes. His wife tried to dry them with a tissue, but in vain. The crying got more intense. The president started sobbing and shivering.

The White House doctor was called to his bedside. He gave him a sedative administered intravenously, and the president became calm but in appearance only.

After a long silence, he opened his heart to himself in a monologue that should make everyone think.

Monologue of the Ousted President

Why did I become president? It would have been better for me to live my life, from start to end, in total anonymity and die in a pale and monotonous room. I climbed the highest mountains just to quickly and unwillingly fall flat.

I'm ashamed when I look at my face in a mirror. The person I see scares me. Ugliness has corrupted my beauty of yesteryear. I became a monster whose ferocity dishonors humanity, a human being who turned into a beast, or object, yet I had such a wonderful future.

Suddenly, everything changed. I blew it when I let myself be taken by the turmoil of my manhood. It turned me completely insatiable to the pleasures of the flesh.

It's only now that I realize, if I restrained myself a little bit, I could have been content with my better half satisfying my gluttonous appetites.

She was willing to stop me from jumping from flower to flower to taste their beautiful nectars. And when I saw the signs of my future demise, instead of stopping, I wanted to turn things around and make everyone forget that their president had a weakness for women.

I needed to forcibly extirpate from their minds the memory of my sexual escapades. I behaved like an unrepentant dictator, thinking that power could triumph, even if I used it malignantly. I didn't hesitate to turn myself into a tyrant and got rid of the legislative and judicial powers as if they didn't belong to the state.

I went overboard. I crossed the line showing off, especially since this is a country of democratic traditions. I speak of my reign in the past, and rightfully so. I'm not worthy to be a leader because of my sexual and political crimes. No punishment will be harsh enough for what I did. I deserve it all.

CHAPTER 16

The New President Installed, the Former Arrested

Right after his inauguration, the new president summoned the directors of the FBI, the Secret Service, and the US Marshals and ordered them to arrest the former president and anyone involved directly or indirectly in his crimes against the nation.

After the meeting, the FBI director who was in charge of the operation met with all the top agents of the bureau to brief them on this delicate mission.

He called the chief of staff to coordinate with him regarding the use of the forces in place to smoothly execute the mission.

It was 10:00 p.m., and many big TV channels had installed their cameras and antennas in front of the White

House. Their sources in the security forces informed them of the imminence of very decisive events.

In front of the White House, the tension was at its highest despite the jokes between journalists and some curious bystanders that were there for days now.

It was midnight when the real commotion began with DC police blocking Pennsylvania Avenue, the main entrance to the White House, to all non official vehicles.

At 1:00 a.m., the director of the FBI informed the former president on the phone that he had a warrant for his arrest. He invited him to surrender to the agents that were going to come and get him in the coming hours. He made it clear to him that it would be better if he cooperated with the federal agents.

The president answered that he would call him back after he talked to his lawyer and the White House legal counsel.

"Mister Redlight, your fate is already sealed. You don't have time to consult people. By the way, this is just a courtesy call, to prevent you from being publicly shamed. How you surrender will depend on you. We can do this in an honorable way, given that you're a former president, or we can treat you like a common individual."

"But, don't I have the right to negotiate my surrender, as a citizen? I need to get my affairs in order. You have to understand, I'm not just like a regular Joe."

"OK, Mister Redlight, we'll see."

The director of the FBI called his colleague from the Secret Service, who had already given instructions to his agents inside the White House, to inform them that the operations will be starting in four hours.

It was 4:00 a.m., and while a cold wind blew over Washington, the journalists parking in front of the White House saw a procession of various kinds of vehicles moving slowly towards Pennsylvania Avenue and the White House.

At the gate, the guards let them in without hesitation. They were met with no resistance inside the presidential palace, and quite the contrary, the entire security staff of the White House joined them.

Washington's former great found himself almost alone—abandoned by everyone. Only his wife and a few loyal servants stayed with him. Looking at the window, he saw the arrival of the impressive procession. There were heavily armed special agents in position on the floor with their weapons pointed at his window.

The White House was surrounded. He retired to his room with his wife to tell her how much he loved her and assured her that he would prevail and what was going on was nothing but an administrative formality, and she had nothing to fear.

Meanwhile, the White House was flooded with agents from all security services, the FBI, the Marshals Service, the Secret Service, and the Washington District police, in addition to members who were already on site with their guns ready.

They handcuffed everyone they found inside the White House while a special commando burst into the room where John Redlight and his wife were.

They forced him to lie on the floor to put him in handcuffs. Right after his arrest, they took him to the Oval Office where he used to address the nation.

They read him his rights like any prisoner under the law, and they let journalists present questioned him.

Photographers rushed over him, the clicking cameras making a deafening noise. He wished he could cover his ears, but he couldn't since his hands were cuffed. His eardrums were extremely hurting. He could not take it any longer. He cried for help.

The cameras flashed, hitting his eyes quickly and brutally. He was agonizing due to the fact that he had not slept for days. This might cause him eye anomalies, or even blindness, in addition to turning him deaf. He would hardly lift his head but was still photographed from all angles.

His face was tortured. He showed his regrets in a nonverbal way, with body language and facial expressions that spoke volumes.

Sadness darkened is worried face. One could understand his regrets, his humiliation, his debasement in being dethroned in the most abject manner. He was miserable and dishonored.

A journalist kept insisting and finally managed to get him to talk.

"Mister former president, what led to this decline?"

"Chasing skirts."

"Did you not know that everyone, especially the commander in chief, must resist the forbidden fruit?"

"You're right. Above all, I am human, therefore nothing of that which is human is alien to me. Whenever I see a woman, I can't help but stare at her."

"You undress her with your eyes?"

"If she is within my reach, I would not hesitate to combine thought with action."

"Is that what happened to you?"

"In these ecstatic moments, I'm no longer head of state. On the contrary, she's the one in charge. Having tasted her honey once, I would want to taste it again and again, multiple times a day. In my dreams, I could feel her. Sometimes, I wake up from a dream, only to realize that she was not with me."

"Do you sleep alone in the marital bed?"

"My wife, out of jealousy and to punish me, was sleeping in a different room. I was deprived for too long."

"Was she not right to do so?"

"She was, absolutely. But maybe, if she stayed at my side, I would have been less inclined to chase other women. I thought nobody knew of my extramarital wanderings, yet I was spied on, hence the scandal. To get out of it, I took some drastic measures that led to my destitution today."

Hardly had he uttered that last sentence when he was led outside in one of the FBI vehicles and carried to a federal prison. The crowd had grown outside the White House. Several thousand people warmly applauded his arrest, chanting, "USA! USA! USA!"

They were kissing and hugging each other. It's an extremely happy crowd that was invited to enter the courtyard of the White House to wait for the imminent arrival of the new president.

The Arrival of the New Head of State

A few moments later, the presidential convoy arrived with a roar. The crowd applauded loudly. The new president was invited to get out of his limousine, dressed in a navy blue suit and a red tie. The orchestra of the White House uttered marching tunes to greet him.

He was invited by the chairman of the joint chiefs of staff to review the honor guards, and the whole high brass composing the joint chiefs of staff were present along with members of congress, supreme court justices and the diplomatic corps. Each of the officers saluted him. Standing on the podium mounted for the occasion, he said:

My fellow Americans and distinguished guests present for my inaugural ceremony...

You are all aware that the unfortunate events of recent weeks have marred us deeply and put our democracy to the test.

However, thanks to the maturity of our institutions and the fierce resistance of the American people against absolutism and tyranny, today we can savor the fruits of our labor.

Be assured that America is in good hands. I'm not going to defile the office of the presidency, as was the case with my predecessor. On the contrary, our democracy will only get stronger. Recently, we have been under the yoke of a delusional tyrant who thought he could do as he pleased. He tried to subjugate our legislative and judicial system, when we know their independence remains the only way to get to measures that will promote peace, security, mutual understanding, and prosperity for all.

Also, thanks to the help and vigilance of Congress and the judiciary who have worked together remarkably. The tyrant was removed to give our country, the leader of the free world, a new beginning with more public liberties.

The tyrant has been neutralized. Now, it's for the justice system to do its work to judge and punish the people who have defiled our democracy and failed to jeopardize our great democratic traditions.

To our friends around the world, I want to assure that we maintain our undisputed role as the leader of the free world and that our relations will not experience any change, instead, they will be strengthened to face the new challenges in the world especially the fight against terrorism.

Our enemies and adversaries should know that our determination to maintain peace and security in the world has not changed one iota.

God bless you, and God bless America.

EPILOGUE

A fact that is likely, but not necessarily true.

A reality in the thoughts that one day may materialize in reality because nobody knows what the future holds. Only God knows the past, present, and future through his unlimited omniscience. He is one of a kind.

So we must from time to time imagine that likelihood can sometimes mutate into truth. Therefore one should be careful and avoid the dreaded, the unthinkable, and the non-desirable because the contingencies might be attractive or disconcerting; they only embellish or disfigure existence.

In a perfect world, there would be no crimes or indiscretions, hence the saying that "life is comfortable, but living is miserable."

If all over the world everything was going wonderfully, any head of state, with their subjects and the governed, would behave with kindness, charity, and righteousness. That way we would all be happy.

In this atmosphere of realized dreams, promises of an afterlife, namely the fullness in bliss is useless. Also do not be surprised to see deregulation in human behavior—be they servants or leaders, be they men or women.

Weakness inhabits them since the tragedy of Eden, so the level of expectation regarding homo sapiens is extremely low. With superhuman efforts, we are able to distinguish ourselves from the plurality.

That way, this example of an adulterous president who became a dictator could have been avoided being under the spell of the fairer sex. He became so dependent to it that he decided to fight democracy and benefit from dictatorship—a form of government that must be avoided at all costs, even if it be at the expense of one's life.

That is why we have revealed very little about the identity of this example of an American president. Fortunately, our readers believe that it was impossible, given the democratic traditions of that country.

However, it is possible that at some point, an exceptional situation will confirm the rule. Should that happen, let's not be surprised and let the appropriate measures be taken to turn away from the wide track, refusing adultery and dictatorship and taking the narrow path of righteousness in compliance with norms, especially in the twenty-first century where troubling events unthinkable just a few years before tend to become commonplace.

Therefore, we must be vigilant and keep our consciousness awake and sharp at all circumstances not only in politics but also during every stage in crossing this valley of tears. It is suitable for anyone who's part of a people living freely in a territory, that is to say, in a state that renounces excess to devote themselves to moderation.

This policy or way of acting should be adopted as an ideal to achieve with sacrifices we must consent to do.

If humanity is shattered by so many calamities derived from our wickedness, it is because we are often heading in extreme directions. The right measure will inevitably lead us to restraint in order to impact, through our actions, our passage on earth.

There are ways for the leaders to behave as servants to better administer to the governed. They will feel their interests are in good hands. That way, the subjects will see their leaders in all aspects, not just as dominating forces, but as chaperons that would fight tooth and nail for their welfare, and they will be willing to participate in an honest collaboration for the elevation of humanity.

This miracle will be the work of the entire society. The fruits would be delicious and for the happiness of all.

There would be a hierarchy without subservience, with people consulting each other leading to the construction of the citadel of progress.

Apart from this process, brilliantly quoted here, it is regression to banish through mutual understanding, where each group performs its task under the leadership, not the dictatorship, of a collaborator who at one point plays the role of a guide.

A new situation or philosophy to advocate and promote through broadcast media, print, television, Internet, smart phones, and especially by word of mouth is the need for our leaders to be aware of their duties. They need to be real shepherds, not intransigent leaders.

The collective interest should be favored versus the petty interests in governance through all the arteries of the administration. That way, we will be amazed at the results, which will be satisfactory beyond expectations.

Let's work hand in hand, and everyone be in favor of the apprehension of knowledge, renewed and enhanced to contribute, within its sphere of action to promote elevation. With the spreading of the idea of putting oneself at the service of others, the world will become a heaven, not in its fullness, but rather as a foretaste of a long-awaited beginning of felicity.

END

Printed in the United States
By Bookmasters